THE LOYAL FRIEND

THE LOYAL FRIEND

UNSTOPPABLE LIV BEAUFONT™ BOOK 5

SARAH NOFFKE

MICHAEL ANDERLE

DISRUPTIVE IMAGINATION

LMBPN Publishing
PMB 196, 2540 South Maryland Pkwy
Las Vegas, NV 89109

First US Edition, April 2019
Version 1.02, February 2021
ISBN: 978-1-64202-224-7

THE LOYAL FRIEND TEAM

Thanks to the JIT Readers

Crystal Wren
Peter Manis
Micky Cocker
John Ashmore
Jeff Eaton
Kelly O'Donnell
Misty Roa
Larry Omans
Angel LaVey

If I've missed anyone, please let me know!

Editor
The Skyhunter Editing Team

For Trudy.
The first day we met, you called me a tiger.
Still my favorite college class ever. And the one that flamed my
fire for writing.
— Sarah

To Family, Friends and
Those Who Love
to Read.
May We All Enjoy Grace
to Live the Life We Are
Called.
— Michael

CHAPTER ONE

Five years ago

There were few things as breathtaking as the Swiss Alps in autumn. For Guinevere Beaufont, only the faces of her children compared to the majestic scene before her. The dark green undergrowth of the neighboring hills around the Matterhorn was enough to make her rejoice. The trees were a dazzling array of reds, oranges, and yellows, and the mountain they would soon be climbing was covered in fresh white snow.

It wasn't the ideal season to scale the mountain that rose over fourteen thousand feet in the air, but the timing was important. They were finally making progress; so close to uncovering the next part of the puzzle, and it couldn't wait until spring, when it would be safer.

Everything would be fine. It was one of those rare occasions when she and Theodore got to go on an adventure together, and although they couldn't portal closer to the summit due to the wards around the Matterhorn, they still had magic. More importantly, they had each other.

"So this fae you questioned," Theodore said. He was only a few steps behind Guinevere, and his breath was already ragged from the climb.

"Elf," she corrected, flashing a smile over her shoulder at her husband.

His light-colored hair was sticking out from under his cap, which framed his face. Ian and Clark had their father's strong jawline, and also his stoic nature. The girls, Reese, Olivia, and Sophia, took after their mother by being too loud at times and always bursting with energy. All of the children shared their parents' independent spirit, or at least Guinevere liked to think so. If she had passed only one thing onto her children, it would be the ability to think for themselves. That was more important than having incredible powers or good looks or all the money in the world.

Guinevere smiled, feeling her chest warm. She was grateful that her children had all of those attributes, too. They were beyond blessed—a strong, happy family with an incredible future spreading out before all of them. But Theodore and Guinevere weren't content with their children growing up in the world they had. Yes, it would be a good life if they did, but it wasn't enough. The Beaufont children deserved to live in a world of magic that was balanced and whole. One day, their children would replace them as Councilor and Warrior. *One day, but hopefully not anytime soon,* Guinevere thought, keeping an even pace as they hiked.

More than anything, Guinevere and Theodore wanted

their children to take over the House of Seven. Not as it was now, but rather how it was supposed to be. It was their dream to fix what had come out of the Great War. That had been a blunt reaction—one man's mission to create exclusivity. A single Founder's fear and prejudice that he spread all over the world.

It truly only took one to change everything, demolishing the House's structure, which had been created with the intention of balance and peace.

It also only took one person to fix things, Guinevere thought. She glanced over her shoulder at her husband and partner. *Or two people.*

"Are you ready to start climbing?" Theodore asked, already out of breath. He wasn't used to the high elevation, or hiking for that matter. Warriors braved the elements, traveling the globe on missions, and Councilors stayed behind and researched. But they'd made the decision that today's mission was a case for both of them. It would require Theodore's sharp thinking and Guinevere's bravery and agility.

"Are *you* ready for the climb, old man?" Guinevere asked him with a wink.

He paused, his hands on his knees as he doubled over from the exertion. "It's true that I'm not as sprightly as I used to be, but I can do this all day long. I'm only taking it slow for your benefit."

Guinevere laughed. "Speaking of things you can do for my benefit, try taking the word sprightly out of your vocabulary. Grown men really shouldn't say such things."

Theodore's laughter echoed in the crisp autumn air.

"Okay, my darling. What would you have me replace that word with? Perky? Frisky? Nimble? Chipper?"

Guinevere grimaced. "You've been hanging out with elves too much. You're starting to sound like them."

"But hey, I'm not starting to smell like them, so that's a good thing," he joked.

"Yes, please never give up daily showers like those hippy elves," Guinevere agreed.

"Or the French," Theodore added, looking toward the ridge that marked the French border. "Do you think we'll make it before too long? I'm hoping to be back by the time the children awaken."

Guinevere shot him a rebellious smile. "*I* will, but I'm not sure about you."

He chuckled again. "I suppose if we're running behind, Ian will take charge for us."

"Yes, he's grown very responsible over this year," Guinevere stated. "One day he'll make a fine Councilor."

Theodore nodded. "But not anytime soon. He needs a chance to see the world and explore before he's confined to the Chamber of the Tree."

"They all do," Guinevere replied, referring to her other four children. "And they will. After we do this, we'll take them on a trip."

Theodore shook his head. "You act like all we have to do is stroll up to the top of Matterhorn and flip a switch."

"And you act like disabling a signal broadcasting to all mortals' minds is rocket science."

Theodore pursed his lips. "It definitely *is* science, and I'm not sure exactly how we're going to disable something the God Magician activated centuries ago."

"Well, the only way to find out is to investigate."

The elf Guinevere had questioned had been in a trance. Breaking into other people's minds without them knowing it wasn't something she liked doing, but she'd come to realize that much of the history they were trying to uncover was locked away in the subconscious of magical creatures who had been on the Earth for a long, long time. They might not remember the events before the Great War or the aftermath, but the memories were there if one knew how and where to look.

The elf had said that he believed there were several ways a mortal could see magic again, the first of which was to be exposed to it in the purest forms. After learning this, Guinevere and Theodore had pieced things together, realizing that was one reason the council, or rather Adler Sinclair, was bent on cleaning up rogue sources of magic. Adler had said that it wasn't safe to have ghosts floating all over the planet, but the truth, they believed, was that ghosts were pure magical energy. If a mortal were to come in contact with one, the spell would be broken for them. That was why they'd been trapping the ghosts and consolidating the magic into the canisters, which somehow always disappeared, and Guinevere had yet to find them.

The elf had also said that constant exposure to magical creatures could, under the right circumstances and depending on the mortal, break down their walls, allowing them to see magic again. That meant that the spell placed on mortals long ago wasn't foolproof.

Guinevere had learned early on that there were no absolutes with magic. No spell would work one hundred percent of the time. Once a rule was made—say, that the dead couldn't be brought back—someone would find a loophole. They were everywhere in this world, and that was what made it so beautiful and gorgeously complicated. Guinevere Beaufont wouldn't have it any other way.

But there was one final safeguard that kept the shield up for most mortals, preventing many from knowing that magic existed. It was the signal broadcasting from the Matterhorn. What kind of signal, she and Theodore didn't know. Was it magical tech, or an ancient artifact? That was also unclear. What the Beaufonts did know was that they had to disable it so they could break the spell. Then, one by one, mortals all over the world would see magic for the first time in their lives.

After that, Guinevere would find the mortal Seven and bring them back into the House where they belonged.

It had been hard for her to believe that one man had started a war until she remembered the history books surrounding other, similar wars. Often two sides fought because they feared each other, or thought they were better than the other. Religion spurred wars. Greed and self-preservation were the cause of many battles. What had happened between the mortals and magicians wasn't so different than the other wars that had been fought over the centuries. It was only different in that the defeated had been banned from a place that should have been their birthright, and the whole history had been erased because what couldn't be remembered, couldn't be questioned.

Now the magical creatures and mortals were separate and seemingly meant to be apart, but Guinevere knew better. She'd felt it from an early age. The divide wasn't natural. It was the result of one man's agenda. His fears, and his prejudice.

The path up the mountain had narrowed, and the terrain suddenly got steeper. Sharp rocks crunched underfoot, and Theodore's breath grew louder. Soon they'd have to pull out the ropes and climb, but he'd do well. Guinevere would help him. They'd help each other. Since the moment she'd met the man now at her back, she'd known she'd found her soul mate. The one person who made her stronger, kept the fire in her burning hot, and made her feel unstoppable. Before Theodore's father and mother had stepped down as Warrior and Councilor, he and Guinevere had been an incredible team. However, once she took her role in the House of Seven alongside her husband, they had forged a bond unlike any other.

There was no place she wouldn't follow Theodore Beaufont, and there was nothing she wouldn't face to protect him. That was the kind of love that made magic seem ordinary. It burned brighter than anything else in the world.

Guinevere sensed the presence seconds before she heard it. Halting, she pulled Inexorabilis from its sheath. The sword was light in her hands, an extension of her, imbued with a unique magic she'd relied on many times. It was the reason she still stood there, ready to face down another potential enemy.

She should have been prepared for the sight of the man who stepped out from behind the rocks, blocking their path up the Matterhorn. However, as much as they'd discovered about the secrets surrounding the House, Guinevere still didn't want to believe that Adler Sinclair was behind everything. Yes, the God Magician had been the instigator, and she kept telling herself that Adler was only a pawn. Maybe he didn't even know anything. Maybe they'd only imagined that the many strange and suspicious things he did were related to his ploy to control things. Maybe he was innocent in all this.

However, when the magician stepped out, his blue robes billowing in the wind, Guinevere had to admit the truth: he was a bad man.

"Your journey ends here," Adler stated, his long beard blowing back behind him.

"Move out of the way, Adler," Theodore demanded, coming over to stand in front of his wife.

The old man, who had paper-white skin and hair to match, simply laughed. "You know I won't do that. You two have gotten too close, which was foolish, but even worse was that you didn't think we'd know."

"Whatever he's told you is wrong," Theodore stated, his voice clear and loud.

A large staff appeared in Adler's outstretched hand. "He is the most powerful magician in the world. How could he be wrong?"

"He stole that power," Theodore argued.

Adler ground his teeth together, narrowing his eyes. "He took it, which is what the strong do."

Theodore tensed, his anger palpable. "I'm sure my ancestor, who was one of the founding members of the House, didn't see it that way since he trusted him. They all did. They trusted him, and he murdered them."

Adler was undeterred by this recounting of history. "The past is over and done with."

"It's also forgotten," Guinevere interjected.

"It is better that way," Adler asserted. "I was hoping you'd see that. Forget everything, and move on. You don't have to lose it all right here."

Guinevere came around her husband to stand beside him. "How do you think we can simply forget that this is all a lie?" She jerked her chin in the direction of the Matterhorn. "Mortals deserve to know the truth. To see magic. This is wrong."

Adler let out a heavy sigh, full of disappointment. "I was afraid you'd feel that way." He lifted his staff, but before he made his next move, Theodore raised his hand and threw up a defensive spell.

However, nothing happened.

He glanced sideways at his wife before looking around to see why his magic hadn't worked.

Again Adler held his staff up, the orb on the top glowing red. Guinevere tried to protect them with her own spell, but it didn't work either. Before she could block it, Adler's magic hit her, knocking Inexorabilis to the ground. The sword slid down the scree and stuck between two rocks, where it hung off the side of a steep embankment.

"What have you done?" Theodore asked, checking on his wife over his shoulder.

"I've ensured that this will be fast and easy," Adler answered, the orb on the top of his staff glowing again.

"You've cheated," Guinevere stated, standing. She needed to carefully negotiate her way to the sword so she could grab it.

"Those who lose like to call those who win cheaters," Adler reasoned. "I've adapted, that is all."

"You've locked our magic," Theodore fired back.

Guinevere hoped Adler would stay focused on Theodore, giving her a chance to retrieve Inexorabilis. It was their only chance against a magician as powerful as Adler Sinclair while they had their magic locked. Her heart was racing, and every part of her was screaming with fear. She'd faced many dangers in this world, but never anything like this. She couldn't shake the feeling that this was certain death. That Adler had thought of everything. That foolishly they'd thought they were one step ahead of him, when in fact, they had been walking straight into a trap.

"You must know that I didn't want it to go this way," Adler explained. "You left me no choice."

"How did you lock our magic without the other Councilors knowing?" Theodore asked. "Without me?"

Adler shook his head, his eyes skirting to where Guinevere was traversing down the steep slope, inches from grabbing Inexorabilis. "I've never needed all of you to lock or unlock magic. You only thought I did. It was better that way. The God Magician changed things long ago."

Only two more inches and she'd have her sword.

"Why are you telling us this?" Theodore asked, probably sensing that Guinevere needed him to stall. They both knew why Adler was divulging his secrets.

"Because I know you'll never be able to share them." With a blinding flash from his staff, Adler sent a blast at Guinevere, knocking her back. She soared over the edge of the cliff, and the fall wasn't something she could survive without magic.

"No!" Theodore yelled, running after his wife. He halted at the edge, looking down at the rolling fog that blanketed the rocky ground hundreds of feet below. With raw vengeance in his eyes, he flipped his head up, glaring at the man before him. "What have you done?!"

Adler sighed softly. "I've preserved the future for magicians. You can't see it, but this is better for everyone, including your children."

The red light burst from Adler's staff and struck Theodore in the chest. He was powerless against the magic without his own, and exactly like his wife, he flew over the edge and fell through the mist to his death below.

Adler didn't bother looking over the cliff at the two magicians lying next to each other, dead. He hadn't enjoyed killing them. However, he would do it many times over if that was what was necessary to protect the truth. It had stayed buried for a long, long time, and he had no reason to think that anyone would try to uncover it again. The Beaufonts had been an anomaly, but with them dead, the House of Seven could operate the way it had for centuries: ruling the magical world without involvement from mortals.

Adler spun to gaze up at the Matterhorn, unaware that buried among sharp rocks and bits of gravel was a sword that knew his secrets. It knew all of Guinevere Beautfont's secrets. Inexorabilis glowed for a moment in an act of dedication to the person it had served, who was now gone forever. When the first snowflakes began to fall, the sword dimmed, growing cold as it was slowly buried.

It would stay hidden for a long, long time.

CHAPTER TWO

Present Day

Winter in Los Angeles was so brief that most would have missed it. The locals, though, complained bitterly about how they were tired of weeks of partial clouds and lows in the mid-fifties.

Liv Beaufont didn't much care for small talk about the weather, but lately, she had been looking for a distraction. She pulled her black hood tighter around her head, trying to keep the chilly wind out of her ears.

"How much longer until we've got sunny weather again?" she asked Plato, who was beside her.

The two were striding quickly down the sidewalk to Rory Lauren's house. She'd been bugging the giant to open a magic portal so that she could simply step from her apartment onto the sidewalk outside his front yard, but he had declined, telling her that having portal accessibility into her house was unsafe.

"Anyone could enter your place," he'd explained.

"Which means I can too," Liv retorted. "I'm not good at commuting, and that would make it easier."

Rory then explained how most magical creatures disabled portal magic in and around their homes and businesses to prevent others from gaining access. She knew he was right, but she'd been deluding herself into believing that no one would want to trespass into her tiny studio apartment. She'd been able to convince herself of that until recently, but she had too many enemies now, and the list was growing. She was certain she wasn't even aware of all the baddies out there who wanted to bring her down. Recently she'd made enemies of a dozen different magical creatures, all in the name of getting the job done.

"It's not like you're going to put on flip flops and trot on down to the beach," Plato replied. "Why do you care if it's a little cool?"

Liv shrugged. "Yeah, I guess you're right. A beach day would be nice, though. How long has it been since I've stuck my feet in the sand?"

Plato gave her a questioning look. "If you mean since I've known you, then five years."

Liv laughed, but it didn't sound natural. "Maybe I'll take up a hobby like paddle-boarding or something."

"With all your spare time?" Plato asked.

"I'm sure I can figure out a reverse time spell so I can get an extra hour in at the end of each day," Liv reasoned. "Remember that elf I met on Roya Lane? He said having a twenty-five-hour day isn't all that difficult."

"He was also on hallucinogens," Plato reasoned.

"Was he?" Liv asked. "I thought that was just how hippie elves spoke."

"They aren't all hippies," Plato explained. "Although that's the majority, there are normal ones who have regular jobs and don't run cross-comparisons on hemp-seed oil or burn candles that clear your chakras."

"I'd be interested in meeting one of these 'normal' elves," Liv said with a laugh.

"Do you want to keep up the small talk, or would you rather discuss what's bothering you?" Plato asked.

Liv frowned. Of course, he knew. How could he not? Liv hadn't slept properly since finding out the "truth." And now she was going to have to tell Rory about it, and for some reason, that would make it real. Before, it had been a dream she'd been trying to shake off. A new reality that in time would disappear, and she could go back to her old life. However, once she told Rory, there would be no going back.

"If we talk about the weather one more time, I might puke," Liv admitted.

Plato agreed with a nod. "I'm glad to hear it, because it's growing sort of insufferable."

"Was that why you disabled the weather app on my phone?"

"Well, yes, and also because you can simply go outside and know what the weather is like," he answered.

"Yes, but what if I want to know what the weather is like in Alaska or Canada or whatever?"

"It's cold," he replied. "It's always cold."

"What about New York or Cairo or wherever else?"

"You're a magician," he stated plainly. "You'll adapt, but not if you're one of those people who start out every conversation by saying things like 'this is some weather we've been having.' I'm currently working on something to erase all of those people from the Earth."

Liv halted in front of Rory's house. "You really should have bigger dreams and less time on your hands."

"Well, what can I say? I've mastered the thirty-six-hour work day."

"And you're not on hallucinogens?" Liv teased.

Plato nodded in the direction of the modest home. "You ready to do this? Once you tell another soul, it will be real for you."

Liv sighed. "First of all, get out of my head, you creeper. And secondly, you didn't answer my question about being on drugs."

"Didn't I?" Plato said coyly.

"Will you go in there with me?" Liv asked after they'd been quiet for a long stretch.

"You know that's probably not a good idea," he answered.

"Because of the kittens?" Liv asked.

"They are all in the backyard digging holes, catching lizards, or sleeping," Plato told her.

"I don't want to know how you know that."

"I was thinking that it wasn't a good idea because Bermuda Laurens is in there," he said, nodding in the direction of the house.

"Then I *really* want you to go with me," Liv stated. "That women is…"

"Large?" Plato supplied.

Liv laughed. "Yes, she's that, but I was thinking something else."

"She cheats at board games," Plato offered.

Liv gave him a look of surprise. "How very random of you. No, I was going to say rude. She's just plain rude to me."

"Since when has that mattered?" Plato challenged. "Bianca Mantovani is rude to you all the time, and it doesn't bother you."

"Yeah, but she's a snobbish jerk who fastens her high-collared dresses too tightly, which always puts her in a sour mood. What do I care if she likes me?"

"But Bermuda Laurens is Rory's mother, and also a leading source on magical creatures, so you want her to respect you, right?" Plato asked.

Liv shrugged. "I don't know. Maybe. But don't tell anyone that I care what someone else thinks, or I might simply die from embarrassment."

"Then it would seem that you care what more than just one person thinks," Plato mused.

Liv rolled her eyes and trotted down the path to the front door. When she was almost there, she turned and put her hands on her hips. "Are you coming or not?"

"Yes, but only if you remember that Bermuda Laurens is a crazy old woman, blinded by her biases." Plato strolled by Liv, his tail high.

"Noted," she agreed. When she was about to knock, the door swung open as it usually did. She was grateful to see that things were sort of returning to normal. Rory's house was neither messy nor overly clean, as it had been when Bermuda had first moved in. The place looked lived in and comfortable, like before.

Liv expected to find him doing Tai Chi or spinning his

pottery wheel when she entered. That was why she was surprised to find the living room empty.

"You're cheating," Rory said with a note of frustration in his voice.

Bermuda gasped at him, holding her closed fist in the air. "I am not. How dare you? I simply rolled that."

"Three times, back to back?" he questioned his mum.

Bermuda threw the dice on the table in front of them, smiling broadly. "Looks like it's four times."

"Ummm, are you two playing Yahtzee?" Liv asked.

"We don't call it that," Rory said, scooping up the dice and throwing them on the table, his attention absorbed by the game.

"We can't start the game over for you," Bermuda asserted, not looking up from the table.

"I wasn't going to ask you to," Liv replied as she strode over.

"And I polished the other chairs, so you can't sit down," Bermuda continued.

"I'm good actually. I prefer to stand," Liv said, feeling the restless energy trying to bound out of her, as it had been doing most of the day.

"And…" Bermuda trailed off, sniffing the air. She glanced in Liv's and Plato's direction, her eyes widening. "Aristocles! What did I say I'd do to you if you ever came near me again?"

"Call me by my correct name, which is Plato?" the lynx guessed.

Bermuda stood, nearly knocking the chair over. She pointed a shaking finger at him. "What is that lynx doing here?"

Liv glared down at Plato.

"You were warned," he said in response to the curious look she was giving him.

"Was I?" Liv inquired.

"Mum, I know, but Liv insists on keeping him around," Rory explained, standing next to his mum and placing a comforting hand on her shoulder.

Bermuda's glare shot to Liv. "You? *You* keep this vermin around? Do you have a death wish?"

"Just the opposite," Liv responded. "Recently Plato saved my life when I was trying to get away from the mermaid, although I can't remember the exact details." When she thought about the lion who had helped retrieve Serena's body from the fountain, the images were fuzzy in her head. The more she tried to think about it, the harder it was to remember.

Bermuda stuck her hands on her hips. "That's because he's full of lies and manipulations."

"Sure wish I knew what she was talking about," Liv muttered from the side of her mouth to Plato.

"She's still mad over a silly misunderstanding," Plato answered.

Rory and Liv both gazed at Bermuda. "Misunderstanding? You left me in the middle of the Sahara Desert without a transport stone or any other way to get home! If I hadn't made friends with the sand trolls, I probably would have died."

Rory and Liv shot their eyes at Plato, who sort of shrugged. "A misunderstanding, as I said. I was waiting for you by the rendezvous spot."

Bermuda threw her hands up. "How could I find it? The sand dunes all looked alike."

Plato shot Liv a knowing look. "As I said, misunderstanding."

"This is all very strange and confusing, but can we move on?" Liv asked, giving Rory a meaningful look.

He must have seen the urgency in her eyes because he nodded and put away their game. "So you were successful with the mermaid? That's good."

"Well, if by successful, you mean I can never wear a dress again," Liv imparted.

Everyone, including Plato, laughed at this.

When they'd recovered, Rory shook his head. "When would you wear a dress?"

Liv blanched. "I did that one time."

"So the mermaid bit you?" Bermuda asked. "How much longer do you have? Have you picked out a casket? I'm sure we can have a small service for you in the back. Your one or two friends will fit back there."

Liv rolled her eyes. "I was bitten by a mermaid, but since I had recently been bitten by a lophos, the antivenom was still in my system."

Bermuda's sudden good mood deflated. "Oh, so you're not going to die?"

"Not any time soon," Liv stated dully.

Bermuda shrugged. "Well, there's always the adventures of tomorrow. I hear there is a rogue anaconda loose in the sewer systems here under Los Angeles. Have you tried wrestling the beast?"

Liv contained herself. Rory had put his mum in her place once, but she didn't expect him to keep doing it.

Bermuda was set in her ways, and that meant that she was going to protect her son from anyone dangerous—and that was Liv and Plato, according to her.

"I came here to tell you two about what I learned when I entered the Ancient Chamber," Liv stated.

They both stared at her. Now she had their attention. She continued to tell them everything she'd learned since then. When she was done, no one said anything for a long, long time.

CHAPTER THREE

The grandfather clock chimed, filling the quiet room with noise suddenly. This seemed to stir Bermuda from the daze she'd been in, making her straighten suddenly. Rory followed suit, blinking as he looked around the room.

"I never would have thought this," Bermuda said, tapping her fingers on the table rhythmically.

"This is big," Rory said in a hush.

Liv laughed. "And coming from a giant, that actually means something."

Bermuda and Rory both gave her disdainful glares. She held up her hands. "Oh fine. You're not ready for jokes. Still processing. I get it. Let me know when I can make light of things."

Bermuda leaned across the table, talking to her son. "If we say never, does that mean she'll stop telling bad jokes all the time?"

Rory shook his head. "It's highly unlikely."

"Ha-ha," Liv said humorlessly. "I'm so sorry that I'm the only one in the room with a sense of humor."

Bermuda gave Rory a confused look. "I don't think the magician is actually sorry about this affliction of hers."

He nodded. "It's sarcasm. She employs it often as a means of communication."

"I'm standing right here, and I can hear you both talking about me," Liv grumbled dryly.

Bermuda's eyes skirted to Liv briefly, then she leaned down lower. "I don't think it's a very good form of communication. It's a bit deceitful if you ask me."

Liv threw up her hands. "Oh, my God, you guys are the absolute worst." She glanced down at Plato. "Do all giants take themselves too seriously and not know how to take a joke?"

The lynx didn't reply. Liv had been surprised to hear him say as much as he had to Bermuda, and she suspected it wouldn't happen again. Plato had a firm rule that he only spoke to her, and had only broken it on rare occasions. She was still hoping he'd speak in front of John at some point so that he'd stop thinking she was making that up.

Bermuda stood abruptly, summoning a carpetbag and an umbrella into her hands. "Well, I think I know what needs to be done."

"Return Mary Poppins' stuff to her?" Liv asked.

Bermuda tilted her head at her, blinking dully. "Mary who?"

Liv waved her off. "Nothing. It was another one of those jokes. Pop-culture reference. You wouldn't get it."

"Which means you probably shouldn't have said it," Bermuda shot back, lifting her chin high.

"Where are you going, Mum?" Rory inquired.

"Well, it appears to me that there are two important things which must be done first," Bermuda began. "There must be a strong memory charm on the population to have rewritten history. I'm going to investigate this and see what I can learn."

"Is that safe?" Rory asked, worry etching his face.

"No, it most assuredly is not," Bermuda stated. "However, before I was trying to find out what the secret was. House of Fourteen—I never would have suspected that, and I'm certain that without Liv, we would never have discovered it."

"That sounded like a compliment," Liv bragged.

"It was a fact," Bermuda said smugly. "Now that I know the truth, I know where to look for more information. I'll have to be careful, but I suspect that whoever is behind all this is protecting the initial secret by putting guards around that. Hopefully, me investigating the gap in history and the mind charms will go unnoticed."

"Mum, I'm not sure it's a good idea," Rory fretted.

"Oh, I'm certain that it's not," Bermuda said, pulling a hat from her carpet bag and sticking it on her head. "I'll be careful, but I *must* do this. Gone are the days of me disregarding that there is a secret and behaving so as to not be punished. Son, you're the one who must be the most careful, though, since I'm sure if I'm discovered, they'll come after you."

"I'll be fine, Mum. Don't worry."

"That's highly unlikely," Bermuda said. "You know I'll always worry about my Ro."

"You said there were two things that you thought needed to happen," Liv interjected.

Bermuda's attention fell on Liv like she'd forgotten she was still standing there beside them. "Yes, finding out how they rewrote history and hid the truth is important, and I know where to start looking. But equally important is that someone needs to make it so that mortals can see magic again. Otherwise, finding the lost mortal Seven will be useless. They won't believe us unless we can prove what happened and ensure they can witness magic like they used to."

"I can work on that," Liv volunteered. "I had some ideas about where to start."

The worry on Rory's face deepened. "You must be extremely careful. Remember that snooping around got your family killed. You'll have to do this differently than they did."

Bermuda agreed. "Yes, I think you need to appear too busy to have time to care about this mystery. Throw them off."

Liv chuckled. "That shouldn't be too hard. I'm already trying to hack my schedule so I have time for everything I need to do."

Bermuda put her umbrella under her arm to free up her hand so that she could feel around in the pockets of her dress. "I could have sworn I had..." She reached into her bag, her face brightening. "Oh, yes, here it is." She withdrew a silver hair clip with two bumblebees on it from the bag. "Here, wear this," she ordered, handing it to Liv.

"Yeah, thanks, but I like my hair in my face." She shook her head, taking a step backward.

"That is one of the many reasons you're not married," Bermuda said at once.

"And also that whole not-wanting-to-be-married thing, and preferring to walk across hot coals rather than date the shabby-chic dipshits in this city," Liv explained.

"Don't be silly," Bermuda snapped. "Every girl wants to be married. "

"Not Liv," Rory retorted.

His mum sighed, pushing the clip into Liv's hands. "Seriously, wear this or put it in your pocket or whatever you like, but keep it on your person."

"What does it do?" Liv asked.

"It keeps your hair out of your face," Bermuda explained.

Liv turned the clip over in her hands, studying it. "No, I meant what is the magical purpose? There is some magic to it, right?"

"It's a busy bee clip," Bermuda said. "It makes it so that when busybodies try to poke into your business, all they learn is that you're busy and not what you're actually up to."

"That sounds really useful," Liv said, glancing up at the giant. "Why wouldn't you have this on you? Or did you use it back in the day when you were trying to investigate?"

Bermuda gave her son a tired expression. "You gave her the book, right?"

He nodded.

She sighed. "She's obviously too busy to read it."

Liv looked at the giants. "*Mysterious Creatures*? I've been reading it in my spare time—which is sort of nonexistent, but I've been trying. And it's a bazillion pages long, so excuse me for failing the test."

"Two thousand, one-hundred and twenty-six, actually," Bermuda corrected sternly.

"Pardon me?" Liv asked, confused.

"The book," Bermuda said. "It's not 'a bazillion' pages long. That's not a real number. It's two thousand, one-hundred and twenty-six pages long."

"Right," Liv said, drawing out the word. "Bazillion was actually a joke…" Her voice trailed off when Bermuda flashed her a disapproving look. "Anyway, the clip? Why wouldn't *you* wear it?"

"Because," Bermuda began with a sigh, "this clip was enchanted using non-elemental magic, which means it wouldn't work for giants."

"Oh, how can you tell how it was enchanted?" Liv asked.

Bermuda's eyes fluttered in annoyance. "Isn't it obvious?"

Liv nodded at once. "Well, when you put it that way, it totally is. What was I thinking?" She stuck the clip into the pocket of her cape.

"So you're not going to use it to corral your hair, then?" Bermuda asked, disappointed. "Could you at least consider combing it?"

Liv shook her blonde hair off her shoulders, pieces of it falling into her face. "I'm planning to try to figure out how to lift a spell from every mortal in the world so they can see magic again, and you're mostly concerned about how my hair looks?"

"Honestly, I have many other concerns about your

appearance," Bermuda replied. "Your hair is only one of them."

"Join the 'Reform Liv's Appearance' club," Liv stated. "I'm pretty sure there is a formal petition going around to confiscate my black cape."

"What strange friends you have!" Bermuda said seriously.

Rory shook his head. "She's joking. It's another one of her attempts at sarcastic humor."

Bermuda didn't at all look impressed. "Well, I'd better be off."

"When should I expect to hear from you?" Rory asked.

"Probably not for a while," Bermuda answered. "But you must not worry. I'll be fine." She pointed at Plato. "I hope never to see you again, lynx. But if I do, remember that you owe me thirteen shillings and twelve head of goats." She paused, a realization settling over her face. "You don't happen to have what you owe me right now, do you?"

Liv laughed. "Yes, they are in his pockets."

Bermuda cut her eyes at Liv. "The lynx doesn't have any... Oh, that was another one of those sarcastic remarks, wasn't it?"

Liv bowed in an exaggerated motion. "And since I know you enjoy those quips so much, I've decided to supply them even more readily."

Bermuda shook her head and directed her attention to Rory. "Do be careful, son. Oh, and before I forget, I left my drawers hanging in the backyard. Would you please pull them off the line for me? And if you need anything from me, you know how to reach me."

"What's that?" Liv asked, realizing she should have read the chapter on giants in *Mysterious Creatures*.

Bermuda didn't answer, simply strode for the door without saying goodbye.

When she was gone, Liv cracked a smile at Rory. "Seriously, what's your secret mode of communication? Does it involve a beanstalk?"

He shook his head, but a smile slipped through despite his efforts to keep it hidden. "You're so very strange."

Liv laughed. "Says the giant who is going to fold his mother's underwear."

CHAPTER FOUR

The crack of the bat hitting the baseball was a welcome sound to Liv's ears. She hadn't realized how long it had been since she had just relaxed.

"Thanks, John," Liv said, handing the bat to him as he exchanged places with her. "This was a really good idea."

He smiled broadly, warming up his shoulders by rolling them. "Remember when I used to get so stressed about things, and you'd make me take a day off to knock some balls around? Well, I figured it was time I returned the favor. You're working too hard lately."

"I don't suspect that will change anytime soon," Liv stated, enjoying the smell of popcorn wafting from the concession area in front of the batting cages.

"Well, then it will be my job to tell you when you have to take a day off." John swung the bat around, missing the ball that flew across the plate.

"That's fine, but next time, you don't have to close the shop so we can chill and let off steam."

John shuffled his feet, re-centering himself. "What's the

point of being the boss, then? I own my own business for a reason."

"Yeah, but since when have you started to take days off or close the shop on a random Wednesday?" Liv questioned.

"Since I realized that life is too short, and we have to make time to enjoy it." He swung the bat, again missing the ball.

"But you enjoy working in the shop." Liv gave Plato a curious look when he popped up beside her. She hadn't expected him there, but she should have. He hadn't really left her side lately, well aware of the new stresses she was under. She didn't know what had happened between him and Bermuda and didn't expect to get a straight answer about it from either of them. However, she was grateful that he was so attentive lately. Lynxes had a bad reputation, she thought, realizing how considerate he could actually be.

"I do enjoy working in the shop, and that hasn't changed, but a lot about my perspective has," John stated, swinging the bat again and this time connecting with the ball. He knocked it straight toward what would be second base if they were playing the real game.

"Are you referring to me and that stuff I brought into our lives?" Liv asked, creating a quick silencing spell so the father and son hitting balls beside them couldn't eavesdrop, nor could anyone else unseen.

"It's not just you, Liv." John handed her the bat, taking the spot where she'd been. He tilted his head back and forth, indecision heavy on his face. "Although maybe you started it for me."

"Is this about the magic?" Liv asked plainly. "I put up a silencing spell so no one can hear us."

John peered around. "That's impressive. I had no idea."

"Well, that's how a silencing spell works," Liv explained with a laugh. "It's supposed to go unnoticed so we can talk privately."

"What if someone can read lips?" John asked.

"Well, I'd need a different spell for that." Liv squared her shoulders, holding the bat with a firm grip. For a moment she felt like she was holding Bellator, about to swing it at an enemy. The ball soared through the air, and when it was just in front of her, she swung the bat, knocking the ball in a long arc.

"And yes, this *does* have something to do with the magic," John began. "I think for a long time I tried to forget that it had been a part of my life, and that Chloe had been. It was hard for a while when I thought about her, and how she just left me, so I opened the shop and threw myself into my work. And when I wasn't working, I remembered her and the magical world she'd introduced me to and then forbade me from being part of. It was always so convoluted and strange with her. One step forward and two steps back, if you know what I mean?"

Liv backed away from the plate, listening intently to John. He rarely opened up like this, so she thought he deserved her full attention.

His eyes were focused on the dirt, looking without truly seeing as his mind pranced off into old memories. "And recently when you reintroduced magic into my life, I was worried that it would bring back old fears and things connected to Chloe."

"I'm sorry, John. I hadn't realized that—"

He held up his hand, stopping her. "It's okay. These are *my* skeletons in the closet, not yours." A tender smile transformed John's wrinkled face. "But you wanna know what? Nothing happened. Well, nothing bad, anyway. When you reminded me that magic existed, I didn't think about Chloe and the life we once shared. And with that thought came another one: I began to wonder if I had to stay busy all the time to keep my mind off her. And so, I took an afternoon off, asking you to cover for me."

Liv nodded. "Yeah, didn't you say you had errands to run?"

He blushed. "I'm sorry. I didn't know how to tell you that I was experimenting with my psyche. I spent that afternoon lounging in front of the television and reading a book."

"I think that can be considered errands for the soul," Liv said thoughtfully.

The shame on his face disappeared. "Thank you for understanding. Anyway, I was surprised when none of the old worries, thoughts, or fears arose. I was still for the first time in thirty years, without negative consequences. I wasn't lamenting about how Chloe had broken my heart or led me on or left me. When I did think about her, I found myself understanding her plight. Much like you, she was worried about how her life with magic would affect me. However, much different than you, she didn't listen to me when I said I didn't care."

"So you've started to take time off because you realize that you can?" Liv guessed.

John nodded. "That's right. And it's really all thanks to

you. I like working, and I always will, but it's nice not to feel that if things get too quiet that my past will come back to haunt me. I worried about seeing magic again, but then you showed it to me, and things were different than before. I felt different about your magic. It wasn't something that divided us, but rather, it brought us closer together."

Liv thought about that, piecing it together with her newest revelation about the House of Seven, or rather, the House of Fourteen. "John, I wonder what's different about you that you can see magic?"

He thought for a moment. "Well, I told you that I was exposed to it a lot. I think that being close to Chloe broke down some strange barrier for me. She explained that it would take time, but was certain it would work. Then one day I saw magic, and since then, I haven't been able to ignore it."

Liv whipped the bat around, practicing her swing. "Would you mind if I did a little experiment on you? I want to see if your brain works differently than a regular mortal's who can't see magic."

"Absolutely!" John chirped. "Whatever you like."

Liv shook her head at him. "Seriously, you shouldn't be so easygoing when someone says they want to take a look at your brain."

He chuckled good-naturedly. "I don't think you've been listening to my story."

"What are you talking about?" Liv questioned. "I took a break from batting to give you my full attention."

"Well, if you'd been listening, then you'd realize that the person who saved me from constantly working and made me realize that magic wouldn't be my downfall again was you." He smiled serenely at her. "Liv, if it wasn't for you, I might have never taken a break, too scared of my past coming back to haunt me. You reintroduced magic into my life, making me realize it was never the problem. Chloe was. *She* broke my heart, not the magic. All these years I was blaming magic when I should have seen the truth. Chloe was the problem."

CHAPTER FIVE

Holding the busy bee clip tightly in her fingers, Liv strode down the corridor in the House of Seven. She'd reasoned that although it was supposed to be the House of Fourteen, she'd better not get accustomed to calling it that just yet. And honestly, it couldn't really be the House of Fourteen until the mortal Seven were brought back.

How strange would that be? she wondered as she lingered in the hallway, watching the founder's language dance on the golden walls. Since visiting the Ancient Chamber, she found herself translating the language a bit better. It was strange, because before the symbols had meant nothing to her, but now, even without using her ring, she understood it, but only a little.

Liv arrived at the end of the hallway too fast and stared at the Door of Reflection, wishing that she could call into work sick that day. Take another hooky day like she'd done with John. It wasn't only that she didn't want to be assigned whatever horrible case the council had in store for her, although that was a big part of it. The fact that Adler was brainwashing and controlling Council members to sway the votes was terrifying. Liv wanted to believe it was purely because she was a royal pain in his ass and he wanted to get rid of her.

However, there was also the very real possibility that he knew she was investigating the secret truth. Maybe he knew she'd gone into the Ancient Chamber with Clark. Maybe he'd been following her. Liv knew her parents were very stealthy, and yet it appeared that snooping had gotten them killed, although she had to remind herself that she didn't have any proof of that, only an unwavering suspicion. And then there were Ian's and Reese's deaths, which reeked of the same strangeness as her parents'.

Liv squeezed the busy bee pin in her fingers, hoping that it worked to keep her safe from Adler and whoever else. Her attention was drawn to the Black Void, which seemed to be pulsing with a different energy today. Liv squinted into the darkness, swearing she saw a pin-hole of light in the blackness. The more she stared at it, the more she felt like she was blind in a pitch-black room, stumbling toward a distant light that had been turned on.

"Are you okay?" a voice called from behind her.

Liv spun to find Akio Takahashi standing by the Door of Reflection. She tensed when she looked down and realized that she was inches from the blackness, about to fall into…well, whatever it was.

"I'm fine," Liv stated, taking large steps to put her as far from the Black Void as possible.

"Do you want to resume your combat training soon?"

Liv thought for a moment. "Yes, I think that would be

wise. Of course, I'm about to receive a new case, so it might need to wait."

Akio held up a single finger. "I've found that when I was in battle, I was most grateful that I didn't postpone my training."

Liv nodded. "Yeah, I think you're probably right. Waiting to train might ensure that I end up in the big Waiting Room in the sky."

Akio lifted an eyebrow. "I've never heard it called that before."

"I haven't either," Liv said with a laugh.

"And I heard that you have a real challenge ahead of you with the next case," Akio stated.

Liv nodded dully. "Yes, so all the training we can squeeze in would be good. And if you have any secret tactics you've been waiting to teach me, now would be the time to reveal them."

Akio gave Liv a strange look, full of mystery. "I think that if anyone has any secret tactics, it is you. One day the teacher should become the pupil, and you can teach me what you know."

Liv was about to protest when he stepped through the Door of Reflection.

"Is it too late for everyone in the House to start acting normal?" she asked, then realized that Plato wasn't there, or wasn't visible, or whatever.

Liv sighed and stepped close to the Door, getting ready for whatever horrific image it would show her—probably her parents' deaths, or her own impending doom. She was certain that it would be something horrible that would infect her sleeping dreams.

Liv stepped through the Door of Reflection, but the image she saw wasn't what she'd expected. She was frolicking across a green meadow, holding hands with Sophia as puffy white clouds rolled overhead. She halted, breathless, trying to understand the strange scene. Sophia laughed and sprinted toward Clark, who had his arms wide. His blue eyes sparkled with delight.

In the distance, Stefan stood, his long black cloak majestically rippling in the wind. He was joined by Rory on one side, and Rudolf on the other. Liv spun around and around, wondering who was laughing until she realized it was her.

She was laughing, a sound that was seemingly unending. Trying to catch her breath, she doubled over, and realized she was wearing a corseted dress. Liv straightened, and the horror of the moment hit her: she was happy. Unabashedly happy. It was such a fragile feeling, as if at any moment, something might swallow it, taking her world away from her. But worse than that was the feeling that followed: *I have no right to be happy when* they *are all dead.*

Liv stepped through the Door of Reflection with the most horrific realization she'd had since first entering the Chamber of the Tree: she was afraid of being happy. It was an impossible reality. It was wrong. After her parents had died, and then Ian and Reese, she'd subconsciously pulled that possibility off the table. Liv could save the world. *Not that she would,* she thought with a laugh.

She could sacrifice herself for the truth. She could push every single boundary set up by Adler and the House, but there was one thing that she couldn't do.

Liv Beaufont wasn't allowed to be happy.

That was a genie in a bottle that had shattered into a million pieces the moment her parents died, and it wasn't like she was on the brink of some treasure trove, with the new stark reality facing her. It was only that she knew no matter what happened, no matter how many friends she made or whatever progress happened, she could never be truly happy.

The peace that John had found wasn't one she could replicate for herself, mostly because she couldn't fathom being happy when the best people she'd ever known had been stripped from the Earth before their time. Happiness was found in the arms of her parents. Happiness would be knowing the truth while they were alive. Happiness would be doing everything she'd done with them watching her.

What she was doing now was nothing. It was too late, and too little.

"So, Ms. Beaufont, you've decided to join us," Adler said as she stumbled onto her circle, aware that Stefan was beside her and Decar was on the other. All the Warriors were there: Trudy, Stefan, Decar, Akio, Emilio, and Maria.

Not since the first time she'd been in the Chamber of the Tree had all the Warriors been there. It was like some strange family reunion.

Liv found herself bowing slightly. "I've arrived, and I am ready for my mission."

If Adler knew that Liv had figured anything out, he wasn't showing it. "We'll deal with you later." He looked at the Warrior two circles down from Liv, who shared Bianca's snotty expression. "Mr. Mantovani, are you ready to take over the elf negotiations?"

Liv's attention perked up, remembering how Decar had apparently messed up those negotiations by slaughtering a few elves.

Emilio nodded and strode away.

"Mr. Ludwig, why are you here?" Adler asked. "Shouldn't you be hunting demons?"

Stefan snapped to attention. "I'm here to give my report on my cases."

Adler sighed, apparently not buying that story. "What is your report, Mr. Ludwig?"

"I've been killing demons," Stefan answered, nearly making Liv burst into laughter.

The white tiger appeared beside her seemingly out of nowhere, as Plato often did. She turned her gaze and met his green eyes. He was nearly as tall as her. Made giddy by the strangeness of the moment, Liv reached out like she was about to pet the tiger. She had done so the one time. The animal seemed amused by this, bowing his head as if tempting her to do it.

"Ms. Beaufont!" Adler yelled. "What are you doing?"

Liv turned her attention to the council, catching the seriousness in her brother's eyes. She winked at Clark and smiled at the rest of the council. "I was just thinking that it's strange that you call the Warriors Mr. and Ms. instead of giving us the title we deserve, Councilor Sinclair."

The Chamber of the Tree fell silent. The white tiger laid down at her feet, nearly touching her as he did.

Liv wasn't deterred by the look Clark gave her. The way Liv figured it, Adler had it out for her, no matter what. Whether it was because she was a pain in the ass or that he knew she was onto something, she wanted to give him a reason for whatever he was going to do next. Or maybe, she didn't want it all to be in vain. If he was going to hate her, she was going to make it worth it.

"It should be of no concern how I address you," Adler stated.

"I couldn't agree more, Adler," Liv stated, drawing out his name.

She couldn't help but notice the smile Stefan quirked or the laugh that fell out of Trudy's mouth.

She might have gone too far, but that was her prerogative at this point.

"Well, it seems that Ms. Beaufont is bored with her previous cases," Adler stated. "Hopefully what we have next will both satisfy your boredom and also keep you out of trouble, since we all know you have a way of dabbling where you don't belong."

If Liv had wondered if Adler was on to her, she had a strong indication now.

CHAPTER SIX

Was it Liv's imagination, or was the white tiger nearly lying on her? She could feel his weight pressed into the side of her foot, but she didn't dare glance down.

Maybe it had been wrong to egg Adler on when she was trying so hard to keep him from knowing what they'd discovered about the House. However, she reasoned that if she started acting nice all of a sudden and not spouting off, it would be even more suspicious. No, the right thing to do was to be her normal pain-in-the-ass self and cover her tracks better. The busy bee clip would help, and she'd been playing with other ideas to keep Adler or others from discovering what she was doing. If she had learned anything from her family's deaths, it was to be extra cautious.

"This is a case that we'd usually assign to two Warriors," Clark dared to argue.

Adler rolled his shoulders up, back, and down, as if working out tension.

It must be very stressful being a grumpy old man, Liv thought.

"Mr. Beaufont, the council has already voted on this, haven't they?" Adler replied, condescension in his voice.

"Yes, but it's very unorthodox to send Liv on a case of this sort without backup," Clark argued.

"That was what you said about the fae case and the demon-hunting," Bianca countered. "Maybe you've allowed your closeness to your sister to cloud your judgment?"

"Well, he *is* only human," Liv remarked. "Maybe you can give him pointers on how to be a cold, heartless b—"

Adler cut her off before she could call Bianca what she wanted. "I would remind you that Warriors are supposed to show the utmost respect to the council."

"Bot," Liv chirped.

"Excuse me?" Adler asked.

"Cold, heartless bot," Liv finished. "I was simply commending Councilor Mantovani on her incredible ability to show zero emotion, much like a robot." She batted her eyelashes at the woman. "Please pass along tips on how you've managed to cut off emotions while sending your fellow magicians on cases they are ill-prepared for while you sit in your cozy chair."

"That's quite enough!" Adler yelled, slamming his fist on the bench in front of him. "This is the way the House was designed, and if you have a problem with it, then—"

"Warrior Beaufont is right," Hester cut in, making Adler fume even more. "It shouldn't be easy for us to assign these cases. That's the burden the Council endures. I don't think that she's slamming all the Councilors, but rather the ones who show little compassion for the dangers our Warriors must face when carrying out our orders. I've never taken it lightly that we send them out to do things most wouldn't do. And the ones who haven't returned? Well, I know their blood is on my hands."

Adler rolled his eyes, apparently having heard this speech a few times. "Yes, yes, Ms. DeVries, we know that your ability as a healer makes you more sympathetic than the rest of us, but—"

"I also share this burden," Haro said, interrupting Adler. "It isn't easy to make these assignments, and I think in the instance of Warrior Beaufont's current case, we have an obvious divide."

Raina glanced up from her tablet, a strange confusion on her face. "I don't remember voting this way."

"And yet you did," Adler stated simply. "Your memory issues aren't the problem of the House. The record clearly states that you voted for Ms. Beaufont to tackle this case."

"Clark is right, though and usually with a case like this, we'd assign two Warriors," Raina stated, reviewing the information on her screen, her eyes growing wider as she scanned.

"But we don't have an extra Warrior who can chaperone Ms. Beaufont," Adler said in a tired voice.

"I'm free," Trudy DeVries chirped.

"I too have a break in cases and could accompany Warrior Beaufont," Akio stated.

Adler shook his head roughly. "No, we have important cases for you two, as well as the others."

"I think," Raina said, drawing out the word, "that Adler is correct."

This caused both the Councilors and Warriors to stir.

Not only because she was agreeing with him, but also her casual use of his first name. Maybe she was still under his influence, although Stefan had slipped her something to keep her from getting brainwashed again, or so they'd thought.

Raina held up her hand. "Although I don't like the idea of sending Liv on this case alone, the vote has already been cast. However, after the initial part of the case is completed and you report back, then we the council can vote again—and maybe this time I'll remember what happened." She glared down the bench at Adler, who was undeterred by this blatant show of suspicion.

"I second that suggestion," Clark stated at once.

"And so do I," Haro and Hester nearly sang together.

Adler tensed, his eyes turning into narrow slits as he regarded Liv with fury. "Fine. We will reconvene *after* Ms. Beaufont has completed the first part of the case. The reconnaissance portion."

Reconnaissance, Liv thought. That didn't sound so bad. It made her feel like she was a spy. What were Hester and Clark so worried about? Liv was a great detective, or so she'd like to think.

Adler cleared his throat, reading from his tablet. "Now, regarding your assignment, Ms. Beaufont, It has come to the council's attention that the village of Lupei in Romania has recently had a werewolf problem."

Liv gasped, making the white tiger glance up from his nap. *Yeah, it's time to wake up, little kitty,* she thought. *Shit just got real.* "Werewolves? Are you kidding me? That's a real thing?"

Bianca laughed like this was funny. *The chip in her head must be malfunctioning.*

"If you'd taken the Warrior training offered to you by the House, you'd know about werewolves," she told Liv in a snide voice. "Really, if you'd been formally educated like the rest of us, this would be common knowledge to you."

"So sorry. My parents were busy teaching me how to be a decent human being while you were learning how not to act like one," Liv quipped.

She was ready for the glare of disapproval Adler shot her and the seething stare from Bianca. What she wasn't ready for was for Haro to agree with a nod.

"If Warrior Beaufont's education is lacking in this regard, then ours was too," he said, indicating himself and Akio. "The werewolf population was brought under control by Warriors long ago, but that isn't common knowledge. I only learned of it while doing research for this specific case."

"A history lesson isn't what we need at the moment," Adler stated. "Yes, Ms. Beaufont, werewolves *are* real. It would do you good to read up on them in the library or wherever you prefer to get your information from."

"Wikipedia," she chirped, knowing that interrupting him once more would really get under his skin.

Adler paused as if he were taking a moment to picture her death. "As I was saying, the town of Lupei has a werewolf problem."

"Actually, it has always had werewolves," Lorenzo chimed in, finally breaking his long silence. "That is where werewolves originated, and where the strongest pack currently resides."

Adler nodded like his interruption was welcome. "That's right, but recently the pack has gotten out of control, attacking tourists and hikers in the woods. That's against the agreement that we have set up, and therefore your case is to go into this village and determine who the pack members are, but more specifically, who the leader is."

That didn't sound so hard, Liv thought. She just had to ensure she wasn't eaten in the process.

"Once you know that," Adler continued, "you can report those names to us, and we'll assign you the next part of the case."

"Is the next part that they have to go through obedience training?" Liv asked.

Adler didn't think this was funny, although Hester apparently did, her mousy giggle catching the white tiger's attention.

"No. After you report back to us, we'll give you further orders," Adler stated. "The key in this case is to go unde-tected. Otherwise, you won't be able to discover who all is in the pack."

"So don't wear that green dress you wore to the kingdom of the Fae," Stefan said with a sly smile.

"I burned that," Liv retorted.

He shook his head. "That's too bad."

"If you two are quite done?" Adler asked, glaring at the two Warriors.

"He was only advising me about how to dress so as to go undetected," Liv told him.

"What you wear on this reconnaissance mission will matter very little," Adler stated.

"Yes, because werewolves are very sensitive to magic," Bianca explained. "They will sense you a mile away, knowing that you're a magician."

Werewolves weren't the only ones, Liv realized. Most magical creatures seemed to spot her for who she was right away. And when she was on Roya Lane, they all also knew she was a Warrior, and kept a safe distance from her, seemingly on their best behavior.

"That's correct," Adler stated. "Which is why it's imperative that for the first part of this case, we lock your magic."

"Say what?" Stefan voiced this exclamation of disbelief.

"Mr. Ludwig, what are you still doing here?" Adler asked in a terse voice. "I do believe you've been dismissed."

"Locking a Warrior's magic is very unorthodox," Stefan argued.

"And yet, if the pack senses her magic and that she's near, then they will go into hiding since they are well aware that they are in violation of the agreement," Adler explained. "Once they are in hiding, we will lose our advantage and have no way of telling who the pack members and leader are. Therefore, the only way to keep this from happening is to take away Ms. Beaufont's magic."

"Liv should at least have backup then," Stefan stated. "Sending her into werewolf-infested territory without magic is too dangerous. Let me hang out on the fringe in case anything happens."

Hester gave a minute shake of her head. She'd advised before that this wasn't a case Stefan could handle. Liv knew why now. If Stefan was anywhere near werewolves, he'd probably lose all objectivity, since they were associated with evil and he had a strong reaction to that since almost becoming a demon.

"Mr. Ludwig, the council has already voted on this matter," Adler stated, obviously more annoyed by this stand of solidarity than anything else. "Ms. Beaufont will most likely be fine on her own without magic." He flashed her a wicked smile that made his face look all wrong. "That is, if she keeps her mouth shut. Werewolves are notorious for their quick tempers and rage."

"Not to mention that the Romanians won't get my dry wit and sarcasm," Liv interjected.

"Liv, this is serious," Clark said, leaning forward. "We're going to have to lock your magic for part of this case."

Part of this case, Liv wondered. She didn't want to know what the other half would entail. Something told her that she wasn't going to like it, but she'd deal with one thing at a time.

"I realize that," Liv stated with confidence. "I agree to have my magic locked. However, will I experience a surge of power like I did the last time once it's unlocked again?"

The Councilors shuffled, many of them looking down at their tablets to check something.

"Although we still believe it to be an anomaly," Adler said, reviewing his own tablet, "it appears that your magic is still at uncommon levels."

"At some point, you all might have to just admit that she's a really powerful magician and this isn't just a momentary fluke," Trudy said, leaning forward and offering a wink to Liv.

"Again, when did the other Warriors decide that it was

acceptable to interject when they aren't being assigned a case presently?" Adler asked.

"When do I need to have my magic locked?" Liv asked, realizing the gravity of the moment. She was done with jokes, at least for a little while.

"When you set off for Lupei," Adler answered. "Would you like us to lock it now since we're all present?"

Liv shook her head. "No, I'm not quite ready. I need to do some research first, and some laundry." Apparently, she wasn't so put off by the current case as to fail to joke. It would take more than that to take away her spirit.

"Fine," Adler said drily. "But do not put this off for long. Mortals are in danger."

Liv nodded, understanding the severity of this case and why it worried Clark and the others so much. She was about to willingly turn herself into a mortal, so to speak, and enter a vicious area full of monsters.

CHAPTER SEVEN

More than ever, Liv needed the quiet distraction that the game of hide and seek gave her. Usually, she found herself having different thoughts when exploring the general areas of the House of Seven, searching for her little sister. Things like, *Why don't I like sushi since everyone else seems bat-shit crazy for it?* Or *Are there still traveling salesmen, and if so, what do they sell?* And, *I feel sorry for the guy who used to sell encyclopedias.*

There was something about searching for the little magician, checking in weird spots, that helped Liv's brain to wander. She was grateful for the random thoughts that took her mind off the fact that she had to have her magic locked and stroll into a werewolf-infested village.

Liv found her heart racing when she stood in front of the fountain in the middle of the garden. She couldn't get the visual of the gnarly-looking mermaid racing toward her, hungry for blood, out of her head. At night, multiple times, she'd awaken in a cold sweat, having seen the mermaid with her seaweed hair and strange slanted eyes about to attack her. She wasn't the worst monster Liv had ever faced—that was definitely demons—but demons didn't live in the House of Seven where her sister often played.

Putting as much space as she could between her and the fountain, Liv strode to the other side of the garden, which was filled with statues.

When they were little, she used to tell Clark stories of how all the different statues came to be there.

"The centaur once tried to challenge our great-grandfather Vernon Beaufont," she had told her brother in a conspiratorial whisper. "They fought, and when the centaur was about to plunge his sword into our great-grandfather's chest, he froze him into the statue."

Then there was the gnome who had given a Warrior a hard time in a pub and gotten turned into a statue, and the elf who wouldn't stop gabbing about hydroponics and was made into a sculpture to silence him. She'd had a story for each of the figures in the garden.

Studying the faces, Liv felt a longing for her childhood and simpler times. She hoped Sophia had that now, although things were different for her sister. She had grown up in a strange time, without parents who lavished her with unconditional love and affection. Liv hoped that Sophia still got enough attention, although it was hard to tell since she was never anything but happy. The little magician didn't know how to complain.

"I know a few magicians who could learn a thing or two from Sophia," Liv said to the contemplative statue of the fae, who looked like he was trying to remember a bit of poetry.

She marched past the statues of four fairies planting bulbs and mortals reading books, and over to the sculpture of the magician Liv had always called Maximus. He had his long sword out as if he were about to duel, and an eager glint in his stone eyes.

Liv pulled out Bellator, bowing to the statue as she did with Akio before they sparred.

"It's time for you to pay the ultimate price for your misconduct, Maximus," Liv said, pointing her sword at him. Then she lowered it slightly, regarding him with curiosity. "If that is even your real name, scoundrel."

Liv spun, slashing Bellator against the stone sword, but not hard enough to do any damage. Then, as if the statue had parried her attack, she reacted with a block, pivoting on her toes and crouching.

Liv caught the flutter of one of the fairies' wings in her peripheral vision. Since she knew that the statues weren't enchanted to be lifelike, she spun around, lowering her sword and regarded the little statue with appreciation.

"Nice one," Liv said, bowing to the fairy. "I forgot there were only three fairies and not four."

Before her eyes, the gray stone of the statue receded as the colors of Sophia Beaufont took shape. Her disguise melted off, revealing the little girl's true form. She wore her long blonde hair in a high ponytail, with a large red bow pinned at the top that matched the red-and-white-checked dress she was wearing. She curtsied, a giggle spilling over her lips.

"It was lucky you came to this part of the garden," Sophia stated. "I don't think I could have maintained that disguise for long."

Liv peered around to ensure that they were alone and no one had seen Sophia transform. "And did you enjoy the little show I put on for you?"

Sophia nodded. "Although I would have liked to have brought the magician to life. Seeing your face when he countered one of your attacks would have been great."

Liv sheathed her sword with a laugh. "I might have chopped his head off, and then we'd have some explaining to do."

Offering her hand to Sophia, the sisters walked down the long rows of topiaries, watching the birds flutter in the bushes. Clark had already told Sophia what they'd learned in the Ancient Chamber. It was a lot for a little girl to understand, but Sophia was well adapted to deal with it. Not only that, but she had asked questions Liv hadn't considered yet.

"Do you wonder specifically what Mom and Dad knew before they died? How much of the secret truth they'd uncovered?" Sophia now asked in a whisper, although Liv had cloaked them in a silencing spell. "Or what Ian and Reese knew or had done? They had to know as much as you do now, based on the clues they left behind, like the ring, and Reese's message. But I wonder how much more they knew, and what all you have left to discover."

Liv nodded, having felt overwhelmed by this possibility lately. "Maybe I need to do some investigating," she said, speaking as the thought occurred to her. "I could go to the beach house where..."

"Is that safe?" Sophia asked.

"Well, it *was* our house, and the land *is* still in the family," Liv reasoned. The cottage where Ian and Reese had died had apparently burned to the ground, leaving nothing behind. Clark had found them, or rather what was left, but he had been too shocked to properly investigate.

"It's worth looking into," Liv stated. "And if I don't find anything there, I could always go to the Matterhorn. Mom and Dad were there for a reason when they died, and I don't think it was because they were hankering for a hike."

Sophia nodded. "Yes, it makes sense that it could lead you in the right direction. But you must be careful."

Liv squeezed her sister's hand as they walked. "Don't worry. Nothing is going to happen to me. I won't let it." It was a bold promise, but it was what Sophia deserved to hear, and Liv would do anything to keep her word. She often thought it was her pure determination to survive for her sister's and brother's sake that got her out of the really tough situations.

"However, a trip to the beach house or anywhere else will have to wait a little while," Liv explained. "First I have to go make friends with some werewolves."

As they strolled through the garden, Liv told her sister about the case she'd just been assigned. To her relief, Sophia didn't appear worried. Being transparent with the little magician about cases while also always promising to return after each mission wasn't easy, but Sophia deserved her honesty. If she started keeping things from her now, she could expect her to return the favor one day—and it was important to Liv that Sophia be open with her, especially as she aged.

"Do you think Bellator will have an effect on the werewolves like it did with demons?" Sophia asked, watching as a bluebird chased sparrows away from a feeder.

"It's possible," Liv stated, affectionately running her hand over the hilt of the sword at her side. "Honestly, I have to do some research on werewolves and find out their weaknesses and whatnot."

"You could try simply asking Rory," Sophia supplied. "He'd know and could tell you.

Liv laughed. "If I tell him I'm going to a village of werewolves without magic, he'll lock me up."

"Clark has been worried about you taking this case as well," Sophia admitted. "He hasn't said anything, and wouldn't tell me what it was all about, but I can tell when he's fretting about something because he picks at his Brussels sprouts instead of gobbling them down before everything else on his plate."

Liv grimaced. "And therein lies Clark's fundamental problem. He wolfs down Brussels sprouts the way I destroy nachos."

Sophia giggled, pointing to a cul-de-sac where there was a stone bench surrounded by roses. "I've never had nachos. Are they good? Clark says they lack nutrition and are full of fat."

"They are full of goodness, which is why Clark wouldn't understand enjoying them," Liv said, taking a seat on the bench and enjoying the chance to relax. She felt as though her butt sank into the stone, melding into one with it. "And yes, nachos are the best. They may not be loaded with nutrition, but sometimes we have to eat for the express purpose of enjoyment rather than the more utilitarian purpose of getting vitamins and minerals."

"If you told Clark that he might faint," Sophia said

teetering back and forth in the grass, not having taken a seat.

"I'll have to take you out for nachos sometime," Liv stated. "There's this great place that makes them as big as a Thanksgiving turkey. They're easily over four thousand calories, but that's no problem for us magicians since we can eat our weight in cheese."

"Awesome," Sophia exclaimed. "I can't wait to share some nachos with you."

Liv shook her head. "I never said anything about sharing. You go get your own Thanksgiving dinner of nachos. When I go after them, I leave no man standing, and by 'man,' I mean 'chip.'"

Sophia leaned over and sniffed a pink rose that was the size of her face. "Well, then I look forward to watching you take down a plate of nachos."

Liv nodded solemnly. "When I get back from my next mission, I'll take you out. John can join us if you like."

"Okay, sure," Sophia said, but she didn't sound as chipper as she had been moments prior.

Liv pursed her lips and went to stand, but found herself stuck to the bench. "That's strange," she said, wondering if she had sat in gum. Like, really strong gum made out of cement.

"What's weird?" Sophia said, smelling the rose again, her face turning pink to match it.

"I can't seem to get up," Liv explained.

"That is strange." Sophia had put her back to Liv, but she could still hear the guilt in her voice, and it was probably plastered across the young girl's face.

"Soph?" Liv said, drawing out the name. "What have you done?"

"Nothing…"

"Soph?"

She spun around, partially hiding her face behind her hands. "Well, you said that Rory would lock you up if he knew you were going on such a dangerous mission, and it made me think that maybe I should too. I can't have anything happen to you."

Liv understood. She wanted to be honest and open with Sophia, but there was no promise she could make to keep her from worrying. This was a girl who had lost so much. Her faith in promises was probably not strong.

"I know you want me to be safe, but confining my butt to a hard bench isn't the way to do it," Liv said thoughtfully. "It's true that I have to go off and face dangers, but I'm going to be smart about it. I've got Bellator, and I promise that I'll do everything I can to return safely to you, but I can't avoid my missions. One day when you're a Warrior, you'll know exactly what I mean."

"And you'll probably worry about me too," Sophia said, twirling her finger in the air and undoing the spell she'd used to stick Liv to the bench.

"One day when you're a Warrior, I hope the world is a different place, and the dangers are fewer and the resources vaster," Liv said, standing. She gave Sophia a tender smile. "But yes, no matter what, I'll worry about you. That's what family does. *Familia est sempiternum.*"

CHAPTER EIGHT

The hum and bustle of Roya Lane filled Liv with a surprising feeling of nostalgia. It was strange to her that in such a short period of time, she had grown fond of the place, with all its peculiarities.

Smells of strange herbs wafted from a shop where an old gnome woman was yelling at a couple of elves for taking too many samples. A cart run by a rotund magician was serving mini Bundt cakes that increased everything from hair growth to wealth, and across the street from that was a candle shop run by a hippie elf who was belly-dancing in the doorway, enticing patrons to "come and unlock their potential by lighting a fire."

Liv kept her head down and her face partially covered by her hood. She was there to see Mortimer for information, although she half-expected to find Rudolf hanging around somewhere on the lane. He had been there on all her other visits.

"Isn't it crazy that when you think of me, I show up?"

Rudolf asked, suddenly appearing next to her and wrapping an arm around her shoulder.

Liv shrugged him off, grimacing. "It's creepy. How do you do that?"

The fae was wearing a purple tunic, which contrasted with his large maroon wings. The new wrinkles and gray in his hair sort of suited him, making him somehow look distinguished—although she wasn't ever going to tell him that. She also didn't plan on telling him she'd been impressed that he'd given up a hundred years of his life to bring back the mortal he'd had Liv recover from the fountain in the garden in the House of Seven.

"It's an entanglement spell I cast a long time ago, so I always know who is thinking about me," Rudolf said and shivered. "I'm looking forward to when it wears off. Surprisingly, I have many out there who don't think so fondly of me."

"Shocking," Liv remarked.

"I know, right?" Rudolf said. "Anyway, thankfully it only works when I'm in close proximity, and fortunately for you, I happened to be on the lane today."

"Lucky me," Liv said blankly.

"It really is, because I'm rarely here anymore," Rudolf explained.

"You've always been on Roya Lane when I visited before," Liv argued.

"Yes, but that was before you helped bring back the love of my life, Serena," Rudolf imparted. "You see, I was always here trying to find a way to get into the House of Seven even though I'm a fae so I could get her body. I was also trying to understand how the revival stone worked, or how to get it away from Papa Creola."

"So the time you spent here was to research ways to bring back another person?" Liv asked, shocked. "You were actually doing something unselfish? This will take some time to assimilate."

"I'm a very unselfish person, you'll find."

"And really modest."

"Why, thank you," Rudolf said, bowing slightly. "So what are you doing on Roya Lane today?"

"I'm going to see Mortimer," Liv stated. She wasn't sure if the brownie could help, but she trusted him, which was the most important thing.

"You're quite taken with the brownie, aren't you?" Rudolf inquired. "Are you two dating?"

Liv shook her head. "You're insane."

"Well, don't worry, I'm sure he'll ask you soon," Rudolf replied. "Have you thought about getting rid of the hood? It gives you that dark, foreboding, serial-killer vibe."

"In that case, I'll be keeping it." Liv moved around various groups, conscious that they took notice of her as she passed, or at least Rudolf, who was a bit more flamboyant than most. "Why are you here now, if you usually came to Roya Lane to get information on how to revive Serena and she's back?"

"Great question!" Rudolf exclaimed. "The love of my life has a rash from all of our—"

Liv slammed her hands to her ears and shook her head. "Don't finish that sentence or I'll punch you in the face."

He shook his head. "Magicians are so very uptight.

Anyway, I'm glad that I didn't bring her along. If she saw you, then you'd be the one getting a punch in the kisser."

Liv scrunched her brow. "Why would she do that?"

Rudolf laughed loudly. "Well, because I don't keep secrets from her. I told her you're obsessed with me, and it's hard for you to keep your hands off me."

Liv nodded. "Yes, that makes sense now. Did you tell her that when I said I was going to put my hands on you, it was usually to trap you in a headlock? And by obsessed, I needed your help with my family heirloom?"

Rudolf waved her off. "Those are boring details. If you want me to teach you how to weave a story that people want to hear, let me know. It's all about how you paint the facts. I like to use a light brush, and—"

"And a lot of bullshit," Liv interjected.

"Anyway, Serena is at the house, decorating it with her flare and getting acclimated to the current century," Rudolf stated.

"She couldn't come here to Roya Lane anyway, could she?" Liv asked, a thought occurring to her.

"No. I mean, technically she could if she came through one of my portals, but it would cause too much of a disturbance," Rudolf explained. "Most don't think this is a place for mortals, and in most respects, I agree."

"So Serena…has she always been able to see your magic?" Liv asked, still trying to break down why some mortals, like John, could see magic and some couldn't.

Rudolf thought for a moment. "No, she has never been able to. That was one reason I knew she loved me for me. It isn't my glamour or ability to create gold from simple spells. Serena sees me as a mortal, although I've explained that I'm quite different."

"And does she think you're insane?" Liv asked.

Rudolf gave her an offended look. "No, she believes me implicitly. I *did* bring her back from the dead."

"Technically I helped with that," Liv stated.

"Technically, but no one needs to know about that, especially her."

Liv sighed. "So even though she's been exposed to your magic often, she still doesn't see it?"

"No, and remember what I learned from unblocking the memories connected to your ring," Rudolf began. "Mortals used to be able to see magic, but they can't anymore. That's how it's always been...or at least, so I thought."

Liv scratched her head. This didn't make sense. Why could John see magic after being around it, but Serena couldn't? What was the dividing factor? She definitely needed more information.

"So, I have something for you." Rudolf pulled a small stone from his pocket and handed it to her. "I didn't forget the promise that I made to you after you brought Serena back. I intend to repay what you did for me. For us."

"With a dumb stone?" Liv took it, holding it close to her chest with mock fondness. "Thank you. You really shouldn't have."

Rudolf's light expression dropped. "You don't like it?"

"Well, gift wrapping could have helped with the presentation."

"Oh, you don't realize what I've given you," Rudolf

SARAH NOFFKE & MICHAEL ANDERLE

exclaimed. "I forget that you were raised in a sheltered hovel on the West Side."

"You mean the House of Seven in Santa Monica?" Liv asked.

"Yeah, yeah," Rudolf sighed. "Anyway, this handy-dandy item will allow you to call me to your side at a moment's notice."

"Cell phones do that, you know?"

Rudolf shook his head. "This is different."

"Before, when I needed you to explain why you had me retrieve a dead girl from the fountain, I simply called you, and you showed up."

"This is different."

"And a minute ago, I thought about you, and you showed up," Liv stated.

"But again, I have to be in close proximity, whereas the summoning stone works from across the globe," Rudolf stated. "All you have to do is hold the stone in your hand and say, 'My beautiful Rudolf, come to me.'"

Liv nodded like this was perfectly reasonable. "What do I do after I've thrown up?"

He shook his head. "Okay, whatever version of that phrase will work. I swear it's wonderful. Even if you don't have cell reception or I'm in the sex swing in a precarious position—"

"Nah! Nah! Nah! Nah!" Liv yelled loudly, covering her ears again and attracting attention from nearby groups.

Rudolf rolled his eyes. "My point is that the summoning stone will call me directly to your side, no matter what I am doing or where I am. Distance is not a factor."

"Will you be wearing whatever you've got on when I call you? Or in your current position?" Liv inquired.

"I will, in fact!" Rudolf told her proudly.

"Cool. So from this point forward, always have clothes on."

"Oh, you're so uptight," Rudolf said.

"No, it's just that I only have one set of eyes," Liv explained.

"Well, you're very welcome for such a wonderfully thoughtful gift."

"I haven't said 'thank you' yet…or maybe ever."

Rudolf sped up, moving through the crowd away from her. "You will. One day I'll be there for you, and you for me. Until then, Liv Beaufont, Warrior for the House of Seven."

He waved, disappearing into the horde of people.

Liv shook her head, finding herself in front of the place where the brownie office was located. She slipped the summoning stone into the pocket of her cape next to the busy bee clip, sure that she'd never use it. Why would she ever call on Rudolf unless she wanted to rapidly become annoyed?

CHAPTER NINE

The dusty hallway that led to Mortimer's office wasn't a surprise. Liv was used to ducking to avoid the cobwebs and grimaced at the amount of grime that had built up around the light fixtures.

What *was* a surprise was the brownie's appearance when she peeled back the door to his office. The room was still a complete mess, with stacks of disorganized papers everywhere. However, Mortimer was looking...nice. The hair that usually sprouted from his large ears was gone, as were the tufts that poked from under the collar of his shirt. He'd even appeared to have lost some weight, which was probably why his suit looked new.

"Ummm...I'm looking for Mortimer," Liv joked. "Have you seen him?"

He beamed. "It's me, Liv Beaufont, Warrior for the House of Seven. Don't you recognize me?"

She squinted at him, leaning down to avoid knocking her head on the ceiling. "No, that can't be! You're his younger brother or cousin, right?"

He shook his head. "Nope, it's me, good ole Mortimer. I've been taking care of myself."

"Wow," Liv said. "But why the sudden change?"

"Well, you remember the last time you were here, right?"

The smile on Liv's face dropped as she remembered the events that happened the last time she visited Mortimer. "Oh, no. This isn't because that obtuse fae said something about you being hairy, is it?"

"It is," the brownie squeaked.

Liv rolled her eyes. "Why would you take anything that Laffy Taffy says seriously? Not only does he not have all his marbles, but the jar he keeps them in is full of mayonnaise and is cracked."

Mortimer blushed. "Thank you for the kind words, but Rudolf is considered to be one of the most attractive fae, and that's saying a lot."

Liv blanched, trying to figure out what she'd said that was nice. Sometimes she felt like the only one in the magical world who was not on drugs. "It doesn't matter if he's attractive. You shouldn't change who you are because he said that you were hairy or whatever."

Mortimer shook his head. "That's okay. I'd been wanting to laser off some of my extra hair for a while. I won't tell you how often my shower drain gets clogged."

"Doing it out of practicality makes sense to me," Liv stated.

"Also, I have a new profile up on Latch.com."

"What's that?" Liv asked.

"It's a dating site for brownies," Mortimer explained. "I

think I work too much, and worry I'll never have anything to show for it."

Liv agreed with a nod. "Have you thought about getting an assistant? Maybe someone to help with filing? Then you wouldn't have to work so much." She stared at the many stacks of papers precariously teetering beside them.

"That's a brilliant idea," Mortimer said. "I wish you would have suggested that sooner."

Liv tilted her head to the side. "Wait, you have never considered getting an assistant before? You manage the brownies for households all over the world."

"Yes, but that's the way it's always been. There's one boss for thousands of brownies."

"Your organizational structure seems a little flat," Liv observed. "Maybe start with a secretary, and then consider getting a few regional managers. Then you'd have more time to go to the gym or get a facial or take a girl on a date."

He nodded, seeming to like these ideas. "I never would have considered this before, but I realize that I've been stagnant. I'm thinking of sprucing the office up a bit too."

"By dusting?" Liv asked hopefully, feeling a sneeze about to come on.

Mortimer gave her a shocked look. "Time isn't a luxury, dear child. No, I was thinking of maybe installing a window or two. It is dark in here."

Liv shrugged. Natural light would be an improvement.

"That's not why you're here, though, to hear about my renovations," Mortimer said, sitting back in his chair and crossing his hands over his belly. "What brings you to my office, Liv Beaufont?"

She'd thought about this extensively. Her family had been killed because of what they knew, and Bermuda had been threatened. There was someone out there, possibly many somebodies, who didn't want the truth about the House out in the world. However, any way she looked at it, Liv couldn't believe that Mortimer was a threat. Did she need to tell him everything? No. But did she need his help? Yes, most likely.

To survive, Liv was going to have to be stealthy, and also carefully choose who to trust. Maybe her parents had confided in the wrong people. Maybe they hadn't told anyone and had instead searched on their own, drawing unnecessary suspicion to them. It was hard to know, but she believed she had to follow her instincts on this.

"I was hoping you could help me with something," she began.

"Of course," Mortimer said at once. "We're always of service to you. How can I help you this time?"

"You've been serving mortals for how long?" Liv asked.

He thought for a moment. "Well, I've lost track, haven't I? I guess it's been a few centuries. I took over for my father, who took over for his." He slapped a hand to his forehead. "Oh dear, I better get to dating faster than I thought. Otherwise, who will take over for me one day?"

"This is the first time you've wondered about your replacement?" Liv inquired skeptically.

"Well, I always knew that at some point I'd have to figure this all out, but I thought I had time," Mortimer said, his words growing frantic as he sorted through papers on his desk. "But now with Father Time breathing down my neck and all the other worries, I wonder if I've put things off for too long."

"Papa Creola has been harassing you?" Liv asked.

"Who?" Mortimer's face contorted with confusion.

Liv shook her head. "Anyway, so you've been in this position for a while. That was what I suspected. Do you ever remember mortals knowing about magic?"

When Mortimer didn't respond right away, Liv tensed, wondering if she'd made the right choice.

The brownie's laughter broke her tension. "Sweet Liv Beaufont, mortals don't know about magic. They can't see it for whatever reason. I can't tell you how many of my brownies have walked out right in front of them when they were up at an odd hour unexpectedly. The mortals jumped, thinking they saw a bug or a mouse or whatever else, but a moment later, they assumed that their tired eyes were playing tricks on them and dismissed the whole thing."

Liv nodded. "That's what I thought."

Mortimer leaned forward. "Do you know of a mortal who can see magic? Does your John?"

Liv chewed on her lip. "He can, but don't worry, he has not seen the brownies who clean the shop or his place."

Mortimer let out a breath. "That's a relief." A moment later he added, "What a strange fella he is to see magic. Do you think he's half-magician?"

Liv hadn't considered that. "I don't know. I don't think so, though." The idea did spark something else in her, though. John could see magic, but Serena couldn't, although both of them had been exposed to it extensively. There had to be a reason.

Mortimer agreed with a nod. "I don't think he is either.

Brownies have a way of differentiating between mortals and magicians, and I would think we'd have seen the indicators. If he were, we wouldn't be serving him."

If Mortimer didn't know that mortals could once see magic, then her assumptions were correct. Whatever memory spell was operating on magical creatures was absolute. It had erased that mortals could see magic from their lives as well as the history books.

"Mortimer," Liv began, "I want to find out why John can see magic but other mortals can't. It's not that big a deal, but it's still of interest to me. Do you know of anyone who could help me study this? Maybe compare how John's brain works to other mortals?"

The brownie drummed his fingers on his lips, thinking, then pulled open his drawer and rummaged around. Liv thought he'd pull out a card, as he had when he'd sent her to see Renswick, the expert on demons. Instead, he pulled out a package of rice cakes. Taking one from the bag, he began to mindlessly chew, his eyes off in thought.

"Where are my manners?" Mortimer offered Liv one, but she declined.

No one ever had a hankering for rice cakes...or celery. Those were just things people ate to quiet hunger pangs. Too bad she couldn't give part of her calorie intake to the brownie. Sharing a name with a decadent dessert probably made diets even harder for him, Liv mused.

"So to answer your question," Mortimer started, crumbs flying from his mouth as he spoke. "I've heard of an elf who works as a neuroscientist. I'm not sure he can help, but I know he does a lot of research on genetics and brain structure, comparing the two to determine different factors. Would you like to take your John to meet with him?"

"Yes, as well as another mortal," Liv said, thinking of Serena.

"Great," Mortimer said, putting the rice cake down with a look of dissatisfaction. "I'll get it all set up for you, and have one of my brownies contact you when it's been arranged."

"Wonderful," Liv said, backing toward the door. "I really appreciate your help on this. Can we keep it between us?"

Mortimer bowed his head slightly. "As with all things we discuss, always, Liv Beaufont. I know you're working on more than House business, and I applaud it. We don't know what the newest Warrior is up to, but we are secretly rooting for you from our hiding places."

Liv winked at the brownie. "Thank you. That means a lot. Until next time, Mortimer."

"I look forward to it," he squeaked.

CHAPTER TEN

Pacing up and down the hallway in the House of Seven, Liv waited to be summoned into the Chamber of the Tree. For the first time ever, she'd been denied access when she'd tried to enter moments prior. Adler had yelled at her to get out, saying they were attending to private business. She'd stood motionless on the other side of the Door of Reflection, staring at the council members and Emilio and Maria, the only other two Warriors in the chamber. Finally, Clark had said that he'd come and get her when they were done, dismissing her.

She stepped back through the Door, pretty sure that whatever was happening in the Chamber of the Tree was none of her business—and absolutely something she needed to know about.

Since being kicked out of the Chamber, Liv had been striding up and down the long corridor, reading *Mysterious Creatures*. For some reason, she couldn't stand being close to the Black Void. More so than before, it gave her a strange feeling of doom. She wanted to believe that it was all in her head, but she'd asked many people about the space, and none had known what she was talking about. They simply didn't see it.

She'd spent that afternoon sparring with Akio. When they were almost done, she had asked him about the Black Void. He paused, looking her over like maybe he'd knocked her in the head too many times. He had, in fact, but she still had her wits about her.

"Sometimes when we see what others don't, it's because we know what others don't," he had said simply.

Of course, he was going to say something riddle-like, she realized after deliberating on his words. However, she'd seen the Black Void since re-entering the House of Seven, and that was before she'd known the truth about the mortal Seven. She didn't remember seeing the Black Void when she was a child, only not liking that area of the House of Seven.

Liv tried to shake off the strange feelings the Black Void left her with, putting her back to it as she strode down the hallway, still reading through her book.

Werewolves, according to Bermuda Laurens, were not to be feared, as many thought. They were vicious animals who were bred to kill and feast, but so were lions and leopards and bears, and most didn't think them monsters. Bermuda reasoned that werewolves were simply misunderstood. She'd echoed what Lorenzo had said about Lupei being the place they had originated in. It was their birthplace, like many thought that Salem was the magicians' birthplace. That was a misconception, but it showed how strong the ties to places of origination were.

Liv actually didn't know where magicians had come from. She reasoned that information had been lost, along with a lot of other important history. Or maybe like mortals, magicians were just from the Earth, not one specific place. However, werewolves had come about because of a complex set of events related to magic, the rise of the full moon, and men's quest for hunger. Actually, it was much more complicated than that, but Liv didn't think the history was as important as the defenses she would need. She glossed over those details and studied what Bermuda had detailed about defending oneself against a werewolf.

Most werewolves are tame and in their regular form most of the month, Bermuda explained in *Mysterious Creatures*. However, some choose Lupei because it enables them to change every night, not just on the full moon.

Oh, Liv thought. This was starting to make more sense. Why else would a bunch of people choose to live in a cold and oppressive area? She realized at once that her jokes weren't at all PC, and she should keep them to herself. She'd once had a regular customer at John's shop named Andrei who was from Romania. Every time that Liv made a joke to him, his scowl would deepen, and he'd say, "You make no sense. Don't quit your day job. Instead, fix coffee pot."

If the werewolves could change at night, no matter what the moon's fullness, then she was going to have to plan her trip carefully. Liv slumped when a sad reality hit her: she was going to have to travel like a mortal. On a freaking plane! With screaming children! And people who didn't respect her personal space, and spoke too loudly, and chewed with their mouths open. And ate things like tuna sandwiches on planes!

Oh, no! That wouldn't do at all.

She was going to have the council lock her magic once she had portaled close to Lupei, then turn it back on once she was out of the village, which needed to be well before nightfall. Hopefully, it wouldn't take her long to discover the names of the pack members and identify the leader.

Liv turned the page to see a depiction of a werewolf. They looked about how she expected, standing upright like a man, but with legs like a wolf's hindquarters, and muscled arms with long claws. Hair covered the beast's body, and its face was more wolf than man. Liv shivered at the idea of running into one of the monsters without her magic. She was definitely packing pepper spray and a dog whistle. Well, and also Bellator.

Her spirits sank a little lower as she read the next page aloud.

"The only weapon that can kill a werewolf is silver. Anything else will only wound it."

So Bellator wouldn't give her any advantage over the wolves. That meant Liv needed to get hold of something that was pure silver for a worst-case scenario. She was serious about keeping her promise to Sophia and returning alive. Well, and also, she really didn't want to die.

For the first time in a long time, she sort of enjoyed her life. Yes, things were complicated with the House secrets and uncovering the hidden history, but aside from that, she had Sophia and Clark and John, and although he must never know it, Rory was becoming one of her favorite people. There were others whom she considered friends too—a community of people who she actually liked being around. She wasn't ready to give that up and join her parents and siblings in the graveyard.

Again, she remembered the image from the Door of Reflection, and guilt prickled her throat. Liv was on the border of happiness, and it felt all wrong. She knew that her parents would want her to be happy. They'd be grateful she'd found a community. But for her, it felt wrong.

Liv was trying to determine where she was going to get a silver weapon that could work against a werewolf when Clark materialized at the end of the hallway.

"They are ready to see you now," he said, giving her an uncertain look.

"I've decided to not have my magic locked yet," Liv stated. "I need to find a silver weapon, and I don't want to travel like a mortal. Can I call you when I'm ready and close to the village?"

Clark hesitated. "Adler won't like it. He'll make an excuse about why it has to be done now, and he'll be angry that they set a time to meet with you and you flaked."

"That's even more reason that I'm going to wait," Liv fired back.

Clark actually laughed. "You really enjoy making him mad, don't you?"

"It does give my life meaning."

"All of the council has to be present for us to lock your magic," Clark explained.

Liv cast a skeptical glare at him. "How do you know?"

Clark sighed. "Because that was the way it was set up. Without all the Councilors, a magician's magic can't be locked or unlocked. Why would you even question that?"

Liv didn't know entirely. It had just occurred to her that it sounded a bit fishy. "Well, then, will you coordinate with them to lock my magic tomorrow when I call you? And I'll need it turned back on before nightfall in Romania. The wolves turn every single night, or at least they can."

Clark's eyes widened, but he nodded. "I'll do my best to coordinate it, but be careful. I don't like this situation at all."

"We already know that Adler wants me dead or dismembered," Liv stated. "This is just one more of his attempts to get rid of me."

"Which is why you should stop irritating him so much, especially after everything we've learned," Clark said.

Liv's eyes darted to the Black Void briefly. "Honestly, we don't know that Adler is behind it. He could just be a jerk with a vendetta against fun people who make awesome jokes."

"He obviously has it out for you," Clark reasoned.

"And I don't suspect that will change if I all of a sudden start sucking up to him like Bianca," Liv stated. "Remember, it's who I am at my core that he doesn't like, and that's not changing. I don't like his brand of governance, and he knows it. But don't worry, I'm going to return from this death mission and any other that he throws at me."

Clark nodded, not appearing entirely convinced.

"What's going on with the elf negotiations?" Liv inquired. "Emilio and Maria are on that now?"

"You know I can't discuss that with you," Clark told her with a sigh.

"I know that you *won't*," she replied sullenly.

He summoned the cane she'd seen him carrying one

time when he visited her at the electronic shop. It had a lion's head on the top, and the craftsmanship was incredible. "Here, take this. It's pure silver."

"But it's a cane," Liv stated, studying the intricately carved device. It had strange patterns around the body and was shaped in an odd way. "What am I going to do, beat a werewolf to death with it?"

"No. It has multiple properties that make it a great weapon," Clark explained. "I prefer it as a staff, but it can transform."

He held it horizontally and pulled at both ends, splitting the cane in two. Inside it were two blades, that although they were small looked deadly sharp.

Liv's jaw dropped open. "Damn, that's badass! I thought you said there wasn't a sword hidden inside?"

"There isn't," he said coyly. "There are two."

Liv rolled her eyes. "When were you going to tell me you had such an awesome weapon?"

Clark's face darkened as he slid the swords back together, making it a cane once more. They fused with one another, glowing slightly. "It belonged to our father, so please don't let anything happen to it."

Liv nodded, feeling a surge of pride when she took the weapon.

CHAPTER ELEVEN

The town of Lupei appeared almost idyllic as Liv stared down at it from the top of a high hill. Although it was cold as hell, the valley in which the thatched roofed houses were nestled was still green, making it look deceitfully warmer than it was. One might have thought it was spring from the bright blue skies and lush green trees.

Sheep grazed in the pastures, and farmers worked in the fields. In the middle of the town was a tall steeple, and around it, dirt roads spraying out, snaking around the various buildings.

Even more deceitful than the quaint appearance of Lupei was the fact that it was overrun by werewolves who enjoyed feasting on tourists and drifters. That was what the report said, and it made Liv feel slightly better that they didn't go after the townsfolk. However, it made her, as an outsider, a prime target should she find herself there after nightfall.

Gripping her father's cane in her hand, Liv prepared

herself for the next step in this plan. It was strange to her that she hadn't wanted her magic for years and had reluctantly had it unlocked when she took on her role as Warrior, and now she was incredibly sad to have it locked again. It felt like she was about to send a friend away, one she would miss almost as much as breathing.

She hadn't appreciated her magic, seeing it as a burden. As the cause of the world's problems. But now, after becoming acquainted with it, she couldn't fathom being apart from it for long. Magic wasn't the problem in the world. It was the magicians and magical creatures who abused it and used it to control others.

That was why mortals were important in the House, she believed. Liv had been trying to wrap her mind around why the House had been originally set up with both mortals and magicians. Now it made sense, because mortals, not having magic, would be objective, bringing that element to justice, which she'd sorely felt was missing. As the inscription on the inside of the Warrior ring said, Together we are strong and balanced.

That was what mortals brought to the House: Balance.

Before Liv had thought that the fourteen stones around the larger diamond on the ring represented the seven Councilors and Warriors, but now it all made perfect sense. The stones represented the mortal Seven as well as the magical Seven. Balance wasn't achieved by having only Councilors and Warriors, but rather by having mortals and magicians. She longed to learn the complete history of the House, and how it came to be, and where it all went wrong.

But first, she had other business to attend to. She spun the cane in her hands, enjoying the lightness of the weapon. It was surreal for her to be holding her father's cane. She hadn't remembered seeing him with it growing up. Well, maybe a time or two, now that she was thinking about it.

Akio had taken the afternoon to help her practice with it, and now she felt comfortable brandishing two swords in her hands. It made for some impressive attacks, although she preferred Bellator. Akio had stated that this was because Bellator had been made for her. When she feigned ignorance about that, he'd simply given her a sly grin. They both knew it was giant-made, and apparently, he knew the truth. It was a good thing she trusted him or she would have had to kill him when he revealed that, although she wasn't sure she could. Akio was an adversary she never wanted to face.

A flash of light at Liv's back made her tense. She yanked the two ends of the cane apart and spun, ready to slice and dice whoever stepped through.

Stefan stepped through the portal as she crouched. He didn't flinch from the near-attack, simply grinned.

Liv caught her breath, rising all the way and lowering her weapons. "Seriously, do you want a haircut, because you nearly got one?"

Stefan ran his hands over his black hair, making it slightly messier than before. "You're a woman of many talents. Demon slayer, mermaid fighter, and hair stylist."

"What are you doing here, Ludwig?" Liv asked, scowling at him. She knew why he was here, and she was seriously considering keeping her swords out to threaten him with. Instead, she slid them back together, enjoying the spark of magic that fused them into one.

Stefan looked out over the countryside, his thumbs in the pocket of his jacket and his chin held high. "Just figured I could use some fresh air." He took a deep breath, his chest rising.

"You might have trouble breathing once I puncture your lung," Liv threatened.

Standing next to her on the high hill, Stefan gave her a sideways smile. "Would you believe that I just randomly ended up here? What are the odds that the place I picked for a bit of respite is the same place you happen to be?"

"Where I happen to be about to go into werewolf-infested territory, you meant to say."

Stefan's mouth opened in pretend-shock. "What? *That's* the case you're on? I had no idea."

"Sure, sure," Liv said, crossing her arms over her chest.

"Seriously, that whole werewolf-hunt-with-your-magic-being-locked-thing totally skipped my mind."

"You're a bad liar," Liv fired back.

"Okay, fine," Stefan acquiesced, turning to face her directly. "Sue me. I came to help. Look, I'm here, and I'm not affected by the werewolves and their apparent inherent evil."

"Yes, but there are a few other problems," Liv began. "The first is that we don't know if they stay confined to the village or if one of them could stroll up here. Then you might not be able to control your evil allergy. If you take out a werewolf because you lack self-control, the whole pack will disperse, and you'll ruin my mission."

"I'm taking offense to pretty much everything you just said," Stefan said with a smile in his voice.

"So be it."

"I have self-control," he argued.

"Yeah? How many demons have you killed?"

"This month?" he asked. "The number isn't that impressive."

"No, just today?"

"Oh…" His blue eyes slid away, pretending to study the hillside. He ran his hand over his mouth and muttered something.

"Did you say two?" Liv asked.

He shook his head. "Ten."

Liv whistled. "And all before lunch. That's impressive, but my point remains. You are compelled to stamp out evil. It's not something you can control. The best you can do is pull yourself away from it at times. But this case isn't right for you. I've got to tolerate the werewolves in order to search out the pack members. We both know you'd complicate things."

"I'd never want to ruin your mission," Stefan said, remorse seeping into his voice.

"Well, that's the other problem with you showing up," Liv stated. "This is *my* mission, and I don't need you holding my hand or watching my back. How did you even find my location?"

"I took a peek at Raina's report on her codex," he admitted. "It happened to be opened to your mission and had the coordinates for your portal."

"How very convenient." Liv pulled out her own device, glancing at the time. "Actually, the council is waiting for me to call so they can lock my magic."

"I know," Stefan said, his voice low. "And I know you don't need me holding your hand. Not even close. It's just that this mission is so unorthodox, and usually, a Warrior would have backup."

"But I'll be fine," Liv argued.

"Adler has it out for you, the same way he had it out for me when he assigned me my first demon case."

"I know," Liv nearly yelled, frustrated by talking about the same thing with people. "But what did you do? Did you complain? Did you whine? Or did you go out there and prove that no matter what intimidation he threw your way, you weren't going to be deterred?"

Stefan was silent for a moment, studying her. "I get it," he finally said.

"I appreciate that you want to help," Liv stated. "And with demon hunting, that made sense. However, this case is different. It's not suited to you. The best thing you can do is leave me to do my job and have a little confidence that I'll do it right."

He pressed his hand to his chest and bowed his head slightly. "I realize now that I've given you the wrong impression. It isn't that I worry that you need protecting or don't think you'll do the job right. It's just that I sensed I could make your life easier by helping. I'm sorry for over-stepping boundaries."

Liv wanted to be mad at him, but it was difficult, especially with the apologetic look he was giving her. "You're good at skirting those boundaries, aren't you?" she teased.

"Well, I realize I was supposed to stop following you, and I have, but in this instance, I only showed up to see if maybe you thought I could be of assistance."

"Stefan…" she said, her voice edged.

He held up his hands. "I remember, I'm allergic to evil.

I'll admit it's hard to control at times, but I'm hopeful that I'll get it under control at some point."

Liv nodded, knowing that if he didn't, it would exhaust him. As Renswick had said, trying to stomp out all the evil in the world was an impossible job that would end a man. "Are you going demon-hunting for the rest of the day? Make it an even dozen?"

Stefan shook his head. "I think I'll take the rest of the day off. I hear there's a spa up in Iceland with thermal pools."

Liv lifted an eyebrow, waiting for the joke.

"Hey, I told you I was trying," Stefan admitted after a long moment. "I know I can't keep going nonstop or it will possess me. Besides, the council will get suspicious if I take out too many demons at once. No one but you and Hester knows that I can track demons easily due to the bite."

Or that he had super-speed and strength as well, Liv thought.

"Just be careful around tourists," Liv stated. "They can be pure evil incarnate when they want to be."

Stefan laughed. "Oh, don't I know. I tracked a demon into Disney World and got confused for a bit. I didn't know whether to go after the demon or mow down the jerks meandering the wrong way on the thoroughfare, chatting on their cellphones, eating funnel cakes, and taking up entirely too much room."

Liv regarded Stefan like he was an alien who had just been beamed down from outer space. Reading the strange expression on her face, he looked down at his chest, as if expecting to see a big stain there. "What? What did I say?"

Liv shook her head. "You said all the right things."

Stefan laughed. "You appreciate my general distaste for most people, do you?"

"I do," she admitted. "I find it beautifully ironic that our job is to protect the population when we can't stand most of those people."

Stefan sighed dramatically. "Yes, it's a thankless job, and most don't deserve to be saved, and yet we are so great that we do it anyway."

Liv shook her head. "Okay, you've gone too far now with your giant ego and lack of modesty."

"Yeah, I know. But hey, I'm glad we can share our general annoyance regarding the human race."

Right then, Liv had the impulse to tell Stefan about the House of Fourteen. The urge was so strong that she nearly caved, but she eventually found the willpower to resist. Telling more people was dangerous, and she didn't need Stefan's help with things. Not with the werewolf case, or with restoring the House of Fourteen. At least, not yet. Hopefully not ever.

"I'll leave you to it," Stefan finally said, breaking the silence and pulling Liv back to reality. He created a portal, giving her one last look over his shoulder.

"Enjoy your spa day," Liv said, waving to Stefan as she pulled out her cellphone.

CHAPTER TWELVE

A s Liv strode down the hill into the village of Lupei, she felt as though she were naked. It wasn't because she'd sent her cape and Bellator to her apartment in LA right before calling Clark, knowing that both would mark her as a magician. Without magic, Liv felt bare and raw, unlike herself.

The council had locked her magic minutes after she'd called Clark from the hilltop. At first, Liv hadn't experienced anything, then there was a giant emptiness in her, as though a canyon had been opened inside her being. With each breath, she felt the hollow ache threatening to take over her.

Liv didn't know how she'd gone five years without her magic, but when she thought about it, the pain of her parents' death had been all she could feel for the longest time, so she hadn't known the difference. Magic, she realized now, completed her. Without it, it was as though one of her limbs had been chopped off.

Brushing her hands over her arms, Liv tried to encourage warmth into her extremities, feeling the deep penetrating cold as the winds swept over the hills.

The council was on call to activate her magic when she called later that day. She'd hoped this would be a fast investigation, but in truth, she had no idea what she was walking into as she set foot in Lupei.

One thing was clear: there was no Starbucks in this town. Actually, as Liv trotted down the dirt road she guessed was the main thoroughfare, she felt as though she'd stepped back in time.

As soon as she'd entered the village, the colors of her clothes seemed to wash away, making her blend with the muted tones of the buildings.

Down the road, children played, kicking a can and brandishing sticks as if at swordplay. However, they didn't make the same noises as cheerful children. Instead, they sounded serious, calling to each other in flat tones.

Knowing that she couldn't wear her cape and hide the cane under it, Liv had decided to use it, hobbling through the town with a fake limp. She figured that this would make her even more approachable, since people wouldn't be threatened by her. But she might also appear to be easy prey for werewolves, which was why she needed to be out of the town before nightfall. That shouldn't be a problem if she worked fast.

The sound of a vehicle caught Liv's attention and she spun around to see a tour bus barreling down the road behind her, kicking up dust. Swerving off the road, Liv watched as it passed, stopping in front of a row of buildings.

From a distance, she noticed as people with backpacks and plush jackets disembarked, talking excitedly as they gazed around the lackluster town. *Tourists,* Liv thought. Apparently, one of Lupei's draws for outsiders was the various caves that bordered the area. It was also a hub between some exceptional hiking tours. However, Liv suspected that the pack of werewolves had invented these attractions to draw in outsiders. There were roughly a dozen potential dinners for the pack striding into the inn at the end of the road.

Liv covered her face against the dust the bus kicked up as it headed back out of town. That was the only time it came through the village each day, and it wouldn't be returning until the next day. One way in, and one way out. The werewolves had set things up nicely for themselves in this remote village, off the beaten path and isolated from anything else as best it could be.

Liv waved at a woman rocking on the porch of the general store. She looked like a pioneer with her long dress and shawl covering her gray hair. The old woman didn't return Liv's forced smile.

"Hello," Liv began, blinking, feeling like she was in a black and white movie the farther she got into the town. It was mostly a lot of gray, as if color were banned there.

The woman lifted her chin in response to the greeting.

"Do you speak English?" Liv asked the woman, her eyes skirting to the shop's windows. The drapes had been peeled back for a moment, but when she looked closer, whoever was peering through them had disappeared.

The woman continued to rock, her withered hands

gripping the side of the chair with a strange intensity. She looked at Liv, not saying a word.

"She doesn't speak," a man said from behind Liv. She hadn't heard him approach, and nearly jumped when she found him so close. He was wearing a thick leather jacket, and his face was covered in a heavy beard that obscured his mouth.

Liv took a step away from the man, who was probably her age but appeared much older due to the facial hair. "Oh, then I'm sorry for bothering her."

The man studied Liv with a curious glare, his eyes landing on the cane in her hand. "Claudia hasn't said a word in over two decades," he continued, his sharp eyes shifting to the old woman. "But yes, we all speak English here. Otherwise, it wouldn't be a very welcoming place for tourists, now, would it?"

Liv nodded, studying the man. His jeans had several patches, as if they'd been ripped and repaired multiple times. Maybe he was a werewolf who had broken free of his human clothes at night, or maybe he was only thrifty.

Extending a hand, Liv said, "Hi, I'm Sally. Pleased to meet you."

He eyed her hand but didn't take it. Instead, he motioned to the cane. "You're not with the hiking group, are you?"

Liv's gaze fell to the cane in her hand. "To be honest, I'm not. I'm a painter. I was supposed to make this trip with my boyfriend. He's the hiker and explorer. I prefer to sit on the hillside and paint landscapes."

"Where is he?" the man asked, a strange calculating look in his gray eyes.

Liv dropped her chin slightly. "He couldn't make it. Too busy snogging the neighbor girl."

The man held up a hand—which was covered in red scratches all over, most of them appearing to be fresh. "I don't need the details of your personal life."

Liv sighed, having rehearsed this story several times and wishing she could tell more of it. What was the point in crafting a role if she couldn't perform? "Well, that's good, because I'm tired of talking about it," she finally said.

The man's eyes shifted to the general store. Liv followed his gaze to find the indistinct figure peering through the drapes again.

"I'm Fane," the man said, pulling her attention back in his direction. "Do you have a place to stay for the night?"

Liv shrugged. "I don't. I was planning on staying at the inn."

Actually, she was planning on getting the hell out of there by dusk, but she couldn't say that. Whoever was in the village of Lupei right then was supposedly staying for the night, but Liv planned to portal home.

She imagined that he frowned, but it was hard to tell with his thick beard. "The inn will be all booked up for the night."

"Oh," Liv said, taking a deep breath. "Well, maybe I'll camp. I suppose the general store will have provisions."

Fane shook his head. "I wouldn't advise it."

"I'm used to extreme conditions," Liv argued. "The cold doesn't bother me."

Fane checked over his shoulder like he'd heard something before turning his gaze back on her. "I still wouldn't advise it."

"Well, still, I better load up on supplies," she said, patting the bag she had slung over her shoulder.

The man reached out faster than he should have been able to and gripped her arm, pinching it hard. Liv froze, feeling her pulse suddenly beating in her temples.

"Don't go in there right now," he warned.

"Oh, are they closed?" Liv asked.

He shook his head. "It just isn't a good time."

"Okay," Liv said, drawing out the word. "I guess I'll see about getting a room at the inn. Maybe they'll have some available last minute."

"They won't," Fane stated as she hobbled off a few paces.

Liv turned back, offering a cheerful smile. "Worth a try, though. Thanks for your help."

She'd made it down the road a few yards when Fane materialized beside her again, moving with a swiftness she'd come to associate with Stefan.

"Where'd you come from?" he asked.

"Well, I started in—"

"No, I mean just now," Fane interrupted. "I saw you come down that hill." He pointed to where'd she'd portaled. From the village, it was hard to make out anything that far away, but if he'd seen her hike down the hill, he had better vision than he should.

"I caught a ride with a farmer," Liv lied. "I forgot his name, but he could only take me so far. I've been hoofing it the rest of the way."

"Palin dropped you off," Fane stated rather than asked. "He often brings tourists as close to Lupei as he can, then leaves them just outside our borders."

Liv chewed on her lip, not sure if she should agree or stay silent.

The children playing in the road glanced up from their rudimentary game as they approached, and their faces broke into smiles at the sight of Fane. "Papa!" a girl with dark brown hair and a face full of freckles cheered, running to him and jumping up. He grabbed her, hugging the child to him as she wrapped her arms around his neck and her legs around his waist.

"You're back!" the girl sang, kissing both his cheeks.

He patted her back and whispered something into her ear.

Liv pretended not to notice, but she caught a distinct look of apprehension in their eyes.

"We'll leave you here," Fane said, nodding in the direction of the inn. "They won't have anything for you at the inn, but if you need a place to stay, I have a room."

Liv forced a smile. "Thanks. That's really nice of you, but—"

"I'm not trying to be nice," Fane said, interrupting. He pointed to a house at the end of a lane that looked like all the other houses. "I live there. It's nothing fancy, but it's better than the inn." His gray eyes drifted to the inn, and he shook his head as if trying to dispel a bad feeling. "Don't drink the mead at the inn, Sally. Actually, don't drink or eat anything there."

Liv didn't know what to say, especially when the little girl he was holding locked her large eyes on her and mouthed the word, "Don't."

"Okay, thanks," Liv said, limping in the direction of the inn with the distinct impression that Fane had found out more about her in the few minutes she'd spent with him than she was comfortable with. It was in the way he glared at her, as if he were seeing into her mind and studying parts of her soul.

CHAPTER THIRTEEN

The inn was bustling with activity when Liv pushed the heavy door open. The tourists stood out in the place in their bright, puffy coats. They clinked glasses by the fire or at tables in the corner, talking excitedly about the adventures to come.

Liv squeezed through the cramped lobby, making her way over to the front desk, where a woman was busy studying a log book. She had long, gray hair that hung in locks around her wrinkled face. Her hands were bent awkwardly at the knuckle, and much like Fane, her hands had long red scratches that appeared fresh. Her clothes were threadbare and had several patches.

When Liv sidled up to the desk, she expected the woman to look up, offering her attention. She didn't.

Liv cleared her throat. The woman didn't seem to notice.

There was a bell on the counter between them, and Liv considered ringing it to get her attention. Instead, she said, "Excuse me?"

"We're full," the woman said simply, her voice deep and her eyes still scanning the log book.

When Liv peered over the counter, she noticed that the open page of the book was empty. The woman didn't seem to care, though, her attention solely on it. Liv got the distinct impression that she was listening rather than reading invisible ink on the page. Her ears were large and poked out from her hair.

"I was hoping that—"

The woman's chin jerked up and her gray eyes roamed over Liv, making her suddenly feel invaded. "I said that we're full."

"Right…" Liv said. "Is there a list where I can put my name in case of an opening?"

The woman's nostrils flared, and something dark shifted across her eyes before she glared down at the book again.

"Looking for a place to sleep, are you?" a voice with a thick accent said in her ear.

Liv tensed, feeling the man at her back. He was close—really close. Pressed up against her suddenly. When his breath stirred her hair, he smelled of alcohol and butterscotch, which was a strange combination.

Simultaneously stepping away and turning around, Liv took in the bulky man who had appeared beside her. He wasn't as tall as Rory, but his chest was double the giant's circumference. In comparison, the man had a narrow waist, and like the other locals, he was wearing patched clothing. His hands were covered in fingerless gloves, but she guessed that they were covered in scratches too, which would match the ones on his cheeks. Like Fane, his face was partially obscured by a heavy beard, but his eyes were different. Darker, and something sinister brooded in the background.

The man's gaze dropped to the cane in Liv's hand and he took a step back, narrowing his gaze. As if he'd gotten something in his eyes, he blinked rapidly, jerking his head to the side.

"We're all full," the woman said at once like someone had asked her a question.

The man nodded, a growl spilling over his lips. "I see that. Yes, we're all full here at the inn."

"That's okay," Liv said, trying to sound light, although her heart was suddenly racing. She couldn't shake the feeling that someone was in her head, or at least trying to get in there. Or watching her from every angle in the lobby. She looked around, pretending to appreciate the modest furnishings. The chairs were faded and looked full of dust. The paintings on the wall were coated in a fine layer of soot from the fireplace, and the walls were... Liv averted her gaze, suddenly seeing the lobby clearly. There were scratch marks all over the wood-paneled walls.

"What's your name, sweetheart?" the man asked, his eyes fixed on the cane she held.

"Sally," she answered at once, not offering him her hand. Her instinct told her to back away from him as quickly as she could to get space between them. Get the hell out of there.

Laughter from the tourists stationed closest to them cut through her, gaining Liv's attention.

"Why don't you join me for a drink, Sally?" the man

asked. "Then maybe we can find you a room, if Vera is okay with that."

The old woman looked up from her log, her eyes shifting between the various groups before landing on Liv. "If she doesn't have any baggage, she can stay, Soren."

"I figured as much," the man growled.

Liv indicated her modest bag. "I've only got this."

"Come on, sweetheart," Soren said, ambling through the crowd. He slid gracefully between the groups, despite his large size.

Liv followed, certain that she'd just found the pack leader. He was strong, and had that alpha appearance. The other locals looked up at him as they passed with an air of respect.

Soren halted at the archway to the tavern attached to the inn. It smelled of ash and boiled meat, which was not an inviting combination. When she entered the area, six bearded men glanced up at her from various places in the dark room. All of their eyes ran over her before darting to the cane in her hands. Liv did her best to lean on the weapon as she negotiated around the rickety tables, pretending to limp.

She noticed then that most of the tables were like the locals' clothes, mended in places as if they'd been broken many times.

When Soren passed the bar, he glanced at the waitress behind it, a woman with dark hair and a sour expression on her face. "Get us a round, Carla," he ordered.

She put down the beer mug she was wiping and went to work grabbing the drinks at once.

"Sit," Soren ordered, pointing to a set of chairs that

didn't look strong enough to support Liv's weight, let alone Soren's large build.

Liv did as she was told and scanned the tavern, taking in the various faces still watching her. *Six pack members,* she thought, studying them. They all shared similar appearances, their faces covered in beards, and fresh scratches on their neck, cheeks, and hands. Their clothes were tattered, and consisted of muted shades compared to the tourists chatting with excitement around the room.

Liv wasn't sure if it was her imagination, but the various groups of tourists seemed to have gotten louder since she'd entered the inn. The locals, on the other hand, exchanged shifty glances, like their patience was growing less with each passing minute.

Soren snapped his thick fingers right in front of her face. "I'll take your things and put them to the side for you."

Liv pinned the cane between her knees, pulled her bag over her head, and handed it to him with a meek smile. "Thanks. The hospitality here is really something."

"Don't mention it," Soren said, tossing her bag in the corner, where she noticed there were other satchels, all with shiny tags, probably belonging to the tourists.

When Soren turned back to the table, he nodded to the corner behind their table. "Why don't you lean your cane up there so it's out of your way?"

"That's okay," Liv stated. "I like to have it close. I can't get around all that well without it."

The man seemed to consider this for a moment. "Is that right?"

Carla, the waitress, arrived at their table with a bottle of brown liquor and two dirty glasses. Her expression was not at all welcoming when their eyes met.

"Hi," Liv stated, noticing that she didn't have scratches on her hands like the others. "How are you today?"

Her eyes skirted to Soren before she poured them both drinks. "I'm about the same as yesterday."

"Carla," Soren said, lifting his glass and sniffing it, "my new friend here, Sally, would like her cane out of her way so we can relax. Put it in the corner for her, would you?"

The woman reached for the cane, but Liv knocked her hand away faster than she had intended and bolted up.

Soren and Carla glared at her with disdain. The six locals around the bar did the same, a strange heat in their eyes.

"Oh, thanks," Liv said to cover her sudden action. "I'd be glad to have you take it. But first, I need to go to the little girl's room. Can you point me in that direction?"

"It's in the lobby," Carla said, indicating with her head.

Liv nodded, giving Soren a meek smile. "I'll be right back. Long trip and small bladder make for a bad combination."

His eyes lingered too long on her face before he took a sip and his head turned in the direction of the front desk, which was twenty feet away on the other side of the loud tavern. "Come right back when you're done. I think a room just opened up."

"Oh, that's great," Liv stated, backing away, her heel nearly catching on the uneven floorboards. She recovered before losing her footing.

As she made her way back to the lobby, she couldn't shake the feeling that she was the only sober outsider in the place. The tourists were loud with excitement, throwing back drink after drink. And the locals continued to eye them, possibly wondering if they'd be better with a side of mashed potatoes or port wine.

Once in the lobby, Vera glanced up at Liv, her gray eyes undeniably full of rage.

"The bathrooms are through there," the old woman said, pointing to a dark hallway like she'd overheard her conversation in the noisy tavern.

"Thanks," Liv said, hobbling for the door. "I'll be right back. I just need some fresh air."

Vera didn't seem to like this idea, based on the scowl that ran across her face.

The cool mountain breeze that blasted Liv when she stepped out was a welcome sensation over the stifling heat in the inn. She started down the road, realizing that she'd left her bag behind, but that didn't matter. The only thing that was important was that she had her cellphone.

Fane was definitely a pack member. And Vera. And the six men in the tavern. And Soren was the leader. It had been obvious to Liv from the beginning. And the blood-bath that by all appearances happened regularly in the tavern wasn't something Liv was willing to let continue. However, she wasn't in a place where she could easily stop it, not with her magic locked.

Bermuda's book had stated that werewolf packs were comprised of ten—nine members and one leader. That meant she only had to locate one more of the werewolves.

She limped past the general store again, noticing that the old woman in the rocking chair, Claudia, was gone, although the rocker was still moving as if it had very recently been vacated.

Liv headed in that direction.

The rocker creaked eerily when Liv halted in front of the door. There weren't any lights on inside, but the open sign was still displayed in the window, although the drapes were drawn.

Inhaling deeply, Liv opened the heavy door, starting when bells chimed, signaling her entrance.

She jolted at the sight in front of her, wanting to stumble back over the threshold to the door and sprint as far from the village of Lupei as she could get.

Whatever she'd expected to find when she'd entered this town, this wasn't it.

CHAPTER FOURTEEN

T hree faces looked at her from various places in the general store, their canine eyes glowing slightly. They weren't werewolves, though. They were something between. Mostly human, but their faces covered in fur. Their jaws resembled those of a wolf, with long snouts, but their bodies appeared weak or elderly. Strangely, they were wearing clothes like they were half-dog and half-human.

Liv checked over her shoulder. It was midafternoon. How had these werewolves changed? She'd thought she'd have more time.

Expecting the three strange figures to charge her, Liv stumbled back with her cane in her hands, ready to use it if one of them lunged. She bumped into something.

Nearly screaming, Liv spun to the side, doing a roll and pulling her cane apart as she did, ready to defend herself with her two swords. There, standing perfectly upright, was the old woman who had been in the rocker: Claudia. She fixed her gaze on Liv and tilted her head mechanically to the side and, not at all deterred by the show of weapons, the woman took a step forward.

"You shouldn't be here," Claudia said in a voice that was more animal than human. It seemed to speak inside Liv, making her think that she would be haunted for the rest of her life by that voice.

"I-I-I…" Liv stammered, backing away and almost tripping as she hit the end of the porch. "I'm sorry."

"Don't be sorry," the woman said, twisting her head around to gaze at the inn for a moment. "Just get out of here, and never come back. Forget what you've seen here."

Liv nodded. "I promise, I will."

As if suddenly afflicted by her age again, the woman hunched over, hobbled in the direction of the rocker, and took a seat. She began to sway forward and back, making the chair follow her motion. The door to the general store slammed shut, and the bell chimed briefly before going quiet.

"Put it away before they see," the old woman said so quietly that Liv thought for a moment she'd imagined it.

"What?" she asked, leaning forward.

"Now," Claudia stated suddenly, her single word hot with urgency.

Liv slid her cane back together, and it sealed with a tiny spark.

Down the street, three figures exited the inn. Liv swallowed, realizing at once that it was Soren and two other wolves.

With her heart pounding in her throat, she half-stepped, half-fell off the side of the porch and hurried down an alley. The werewolves in Lupei were supposed to be able to change every night, but not during the day. It didn't make any sense.

And there were way more than ten among the town's four hundred residents. Plus, she couldn't fathom why she got the distinct impression that the ones in the general store were old and more human than wolf—or somehow stuck between.

Liv was sprinting for the edge of the village when she heard footsteps behind her. Someone was running after her. She picked up her pace, carrying her cane in one hand and ready to use it. Not having magic right then was the worst possible thing. There were wolves all around her—she knew it. Could Soren and his gang change like the ones in the general store? What had she gotten herself into?

Slipping her hand into her pocket, she reached for her cellphone. Her heart nearly exploded in her chest.

It wasn't there!

Running as fast as she could manage, she hooked the cane under her arm, digging in both her pockets for her cellphone. She'd put it there right after calling Clark and having her magic locked—she knew it. And yet, all her pockets were empty. Someone had taken it!

Her cellphone was gone, and with it, any way of getting back her magic.

Liv pushed harder, hearing the footsteps grow faster. They were closing in on her, and she couldn't outrun them. They were too fast, and all she had was her father's cane. She feared it wouldn't be enough against three werewolves, and however many were behind them.

She wasn't sure if getting out of the village would help. Could the werewolves leave? Were they unable to transform on any given night outside the village boundaries? She wasn't sure, but she had to make a break for it. There was only one more row of buildings, and then the road. She believed with every fiber of her being that she could make it.

Liv sprinted, coming upon the last set of houses. She was so close. When she passed the corner of a dilapidated farmhouse, something reached out and grabbed her, holding her tightly and covering her mouth.

"If you want to survive," a hot voice whispered in her ear, "then stay absolutely quiet and keep that damn cane away from me."

CHAPTER FIFTEEN

The man's hands covering Liv's mouth smelled of wood and salt. She thought about biting him and breaking free, but something at her core told her not to try biting a werewolf. That was just bad form.

The figure yanked her in tighter, pulling them into the shadows of the neighboring house. Her breath was ragged from running and being grabbed by this stranger, and although she wasn't sure what to do, she did keep the cane low. He'd said that if she wanted to survive that she had to stay quiet, so she held her breath.

A second later, the sounds of running footsteps halted, followed by rustling. Sniffing. A low growl.

"I think she got away," a man's voice called from the other side of the house, making Liv nearly gasp. She let out a slow breath, careful not to make a noise.

"Yeah, I don't smell her anymore," another voice called.

"Let's get back to the inn and report back to Vera," a man said.

More footsteps, then all noises vanished for a moment. When a sheep baahed in a nearby field, Liv jumped.

The man released her, spinning her around to face him with a force to impress.

It was Fane, and his face was deadly serious. He held a finger to his mouth, the universal signal for "keep your mouth shut."

Liv nodded. She wasn't sure why Fane had come to her rescue, or if he'd even rescued her at all. Maybe he was saving her for himself, his own personal meal that night that he didn't want to share with the others. He *had* offered to have her stay with him. However, there was something in his eyes that made her want to trust him. But with no magic and no way to get it back, and being stuck in a town with a bunch of savage werewolves, she didn't really have a choice.

Fane removed the large coat he was wearing and handed it to Liv. She flashed him a confused look and shook her head. The gesture was nice, but she wasn't cold. Actually, from the run and the adrenaline, she was sweating profusely and feeling quite hot.

Leaning in close, Fane whispered in her ear, "Put it on, or they will smell you."

Oh, she thought. That made sense. Maybe that was why they'd quit tracking her? Fane's smell had confused them or masked her.

Doing as she was told, Liv slipped into the huge jacket. It fit her like a dress, the arms covering her hands.

Fane peeked around the corner, checking. Having determined that the alley was clear, he grabbed Liv's arm and yanked her out into the open area between the two houses.

Liv wasn't sure why, because she'd thought it was only mid-afternoon before, but the light looked like that of dusk; like the sun was already setting. She gazed around, and then it hit her. The tallest mountains were to the west, blocking the sun and making for an earlier sunset. She should have planned for this. Soon the sun would be down in a village full of werewolves who could turn every night and apparently made snacks of tourists.

She reminded herself that she was one of those outsiders.

Fane led Liv through the town, taking a circuitous route that snaked between buildings. He stopped every few yards to sniff, his ears moving slightly toward different noises.

When they'd arrived at the lane where he'd indicated that he'd lived, he pointed to a modest house with a thatched roof. Liv waited for him to lead the way, but instead, he pushed her and mouthed, "Go."

Unclear exactly what she should do but definitely out of options, Liv ran for the house, hesitating at the door.

He waved her on, urgency in his eyes.

She put her hand on the doorknob, indecision rolling around in her being. And then the male voice from before rang out on the main road, only two houses away.

"Any luck?" he called. It was Soren, she realized now, catching his accent.

"None," someone replied. "But if she's around here, we'll find her tonight."

Liv pushed the door open as Fane stepped out from the

building where he was hiding and raced toward the main road.

Liv slammed the door behind her, putting her back to it.

No werewolf was waiting to tear into Liv's flesh once she was inside the small house. To her relief, there was only one person in the main room. The little girl from before was lying on her stomach in front of the fire, reading a book.

She pushed up at the sight of Liv, curiously looking her over. "Papa said you were out there getting yourself in trouble. You didn't eat or drink anything at the inn, did you?"

The girl was about Sophia's age, but she was taller, and her eyes were much more mature than a normal eight-year old's. Her thick dark hair cascaded down her back, and she wore a simple dress and thick tights.

"No, I didn't," Liv whispered, searching the room as she tried to get her breath. The space was small and cramped, and its furniture was covered with thick blankets. On the side was a modest kitchen that included very limited counter space and no appliances, only a wood-burning stove and a small sink.

At the back was a cramped hallway that probably led to bedrooms.

"Is anyone else here?" Liv asked the girl.

She shook her head. "Papa and I live alone. My mama ran off with a different pack that's south of here. Papa says we won't see her again, but I don't know. Stranger things have happened."

Liv merely nodded, not sure how to respond to this,

then she realized she was still wearing Fane's coat. She tugged on the sleeve and looked at the girl. "Do you think I can take this off?"

"Yes," she answered. "They can't smell you in here. Papa puts up different things around our house to keep mortals safe."

Liv shrugged off the jacket, suddenly feeling the chill in the small house. Even with the fire burning, it was still much colder in this place than she was used to—a cold that caused her teeth to chatter and made her think it would forever live in her bones.

"Your momma ran off with another pack?" Liv asked, noticing that there were little personal effects in the house, only books and framed embroidery. "Is she a…"

The girl nodded and pointed at the door. "Papa is coming back now. You should move away from the door."

Liv did as she was told, and not a moment later Fane stalked through the door, slamming it closed, and latching four locks into place. When he turned to look at Liv, she stepped back two feet, not sure what to make of the brooding stare he was giving her.

"You're safe for now," he told her in a cautious whisper.

Safe for now, Liv thought. *Does that mean safe until later when he shifts and eats me?*

"Can you please explain what's going on here?" Liv asked, pressing her cane to her chest for comfort.

Fane pointed at the kitchen, directing his attention to his daughter. "Alina, make supper, would you?"

She nodded and set off with her head down. "Yes, Papa."

Fane marched over to Liv and looked down at her with

an expression she couldn't read. She tightened her grip on the cane, ready to attack if needed.

Fane swallowed, his large Adam's apple hesitating in his throat, and his fists flexed by his side. He narrowed his eyes at the cane in her hands and shook his head. "Why did you come here, Warrior?"

CHAPTER SIXTEEN

Liv was speechless for a moment. Alina had looked up from the kitchen, curiosity covering her freckled face.

"How do you know that I'm a Warrior?" Liv asked, unsure if she should deny it. Everything about this situation was incredibly confusing.

Fane pointed to the cane in her hands. "That belonged to Theodore Beaufont. You have his eyes. And if you're here, then it is because of the House of Seven, which would make you a Warrior."

That was some fantastic reasoning, Liv thought, impressed by how he'd pieced so much together.

"How do you know my father? And how did you know this was his cane?" Liv asked, gripping the weapon even tighter, ready to yank it apart if needed. She really didn't like that Alina was watching so intently from the kitchen, but what would she do if Fane attacked her? She had to defend herself, even if that meant doing so in front of his daughter.

Fane took a step backward, giving her some space. He sighed. "I knew your father. I'm sorry for your loss. I heard about what happened to him and your mother. They were..." He hesitated, a strange tenderness flocking to his eyes. "They were better than most."

"What? You knew them?" Liv asked.

"I gave him that cane, actually," Fane explained.

Liv's eyes dropped in disbelief to the pure silver cane in her hands. "What? But you're a werewolf. How...I mean, why? I really don't understand."

Fane nodded, seeming to understand her confusion. "Your parents, as good as they were, made a lot of enemies, but that was only because they tried hard to fight for werewolves' rights. They knew that many of us were honest people who manage our curse the best we knew how. When your mother tried to corral a particularly vicious pack south of here, they took it personally.

"I was worried for your father, so I had that cane made and sent to him. It was my way of thanking him for protecting our village using the laws of the council. I knew the position he had taken as Councilor didn't make him popular, and I was afraid the Bulgarian pack would come after him. Unfortunately, it seems that something else came after your parents, and I don't believe it was werewolves."

Liv's legs shook, and she steadied herself by placing her hand on a nearby wall.

"You should sit down," Alina said, bring a steaming-hot mug to her. "Drink this. It will calm your nerves."

Liv glanced at Fane uncertainly.

He nodded. "It's only tea. I have no reason to want to drug you, Warrior. I'm not like the others."

Liv took the mug and sat down on the straw bench in front of the fire, which was hard in places and lumpy in others. "I don't understand what's going on here. None of this was in the report. Who were those werewolves in the general store?"

Fane warmed his hands in front of the fire. "First, tell me why you're here. Then I can fill in the gaps."

"Well, the council has become aware of the attacks on tourists and hikers in Lupei," Liv stated.

Fane sighed loudly. "I knew they would. I warned the pack they'd gone too far."

Liv blew on the tea, enjoying the warm mug in her hands. "I was sent to find the names of the pack and alpha."

"And they locked your magic so that you'd go undetected," Fane guessed.

"Yes, and someone stole my cell phone, so I can't have it reactivated. I'm stuck," Liv explained.

"You are until morning," Fane agreed. "At sunrise, you have to get over the ridge and hike to Palin's house. It's about twenty miles away. He'll take you to the city from there, where you can reach your council and activate your magic."

Twenty miles away. Hiking through the hills for that long in the cold wouldn't be easy. Liv sorely missed her magic. Never again would she so easily have it locked.

Fane blew out a breath and took the mug of tea that Alina handed him. He nodded at her appreciatively. "It seems as though your parents kept their word and did not disclose the truth about Lupei."

"The truth?" Liv questioned.

"Your council has asked you to identify the pack members and the alpha, which means they don't know the truth." Fane gulped his tea, running his hand over his beard. "Years ago, the pack from Bulgaria came up here, causing problems for us and attracting unwanted attention from the council. It was then that your mother was ordered to come here and put a stop to it. Similar to how the House of Seven tracks magicians, they wanted trackers put on us, but she knew it was wrong. She determined that it was the Bulgarian pack causing all the problems, so she ran them out of town and kept our secret, knowing that the council would do something extreme if they found out the truth. They have never put the trackers on us, thanks to her. To this day, you're the only magician to know the truth about Lupei."

Liv furrowed her brow. "What truth? I'm absolutely confused, and don't know anything."

Fane finished his tea, holding the mug out for Alina to take. She dutifully did so, returning to the kitchen to stir the contents of the pots on the stove. "Your name isn't Sally. What is it?"

Liv blushed, having not expected the question. "I'm Liv. Liv Beaufont, the second of my parents' children to take on the role as Warrior."

Grief edged Fane's eyes. "I'm sorry. It appears that the tragedies for the Beaufonts continue. It is hard for the noble to escape persecution, though."

Liv noticed then that the scratches that Fane had on his hands were all gone. Now they were only faint pink lines.

"Liv, you know what Lupei is, right?"

She nodded, thinking back to Bermuda's book. "It's where werewolves originated."

"That's right," he affirmed. "It was a curse that an incredibly powerful magician put on the town centuries ago. Now it's our bite that spreads the disease. Only those from Lupei can turn someone into a werewolf."

Liv didn't say anything, only sipped her tea, waiting for him to go on.

"When your mother came here, she discovered what was going on," Fane continued. "It wasn't the werewolves here who were creating the problem. It was the Bulgarian pack, trying to get us into trouble by setting us up. She helped us to get rid of them."

Alina looked at them from the kitchen. "That was when my momma left. She liked them better."

Fane sighed. "Nicoleta wanted notoriety, and she wasn't going to get that here where we're all the same. However, away from here, she's stronger than the others because of the curse, and she has the power to turn others into werewolves."

"I still don't understand," Liv stated, trying to piece all the strange bits together. "What's the secret?"

"The secret your mother withheld from the council kept us alive. No one knows that only a Lupei werewolf's bite can spread the curse," Fane imparted.

"So that's it?" Liv asked. "You're part of the original pack that carries the curse. Did my mother fear what the council would do if they found out the truth?"

He nodded. "She knew they'd require her to exterminate us. Werewolves aren't a problem the House likes dealing with. All the other magical creatures would support them in this. If others knew that it was only the Lupei pack that could spread this curse, we'd be wiped out, and there would be no more worries about werewolves spreading."

"Wow," Liv said, running her hands through her hair as she tried to digest this. "It's crazy that a pack of ten are the only ones who can infect others."

Fane's eyes skirted to his daughter briefly. "That's the other part of the secret, which you may already have figured out if you think about it."

Liv blinked at him, trying to understand what she was missing. She'd experienced so much since arriving there that morning that she hadn't had a chance to analyze any of it. She thought of the inn with the brutal scratch marks everywhere, and the locals dressed in patched clothes. Then she remembered the general store where she found the strange werewolves. It all wove together and she suddenly understood, nearly dropping her mug.

"There isn't a pack of ten in Lupei," Liv stated. "*Everyone* in the town is a werewolf, aren't they?"

Fane let out a heavy breath. "Yes, that's correct," he affirmed. "The magician who spelled us made it so that anyone born here is cursed."

Liv glanced at Alina, who was busy slicing bread. "So, your daughter?"

Fane nodded morosely. "Her curse is dormant, as is the case for over half the residents. It comes out on the full moon, but only then. For the rest of us, we turn every single night."

Liv thought of the woman in the bar whom Soren had asked to take her cane. She had to be an outsider.

"And those people in the general store?" Liv asked.

"Those are some of our oldest residents," Fane explained. "They have trouble turning back, something that affects us as we age. Claudia watches them, ensuring that the tourists don't see them."

"Claudia spoke to me," Liv admitted. "You said she hadn't spoken in a long time."

"Claudia hasn't spoken to an outsider in a long time," Fane stated. "I'm surprised she said anything to you, but that was one reason I brought you here. She doesn't trust those from outside Lupei. We've had to deal with so much, and many werewolves who have been turned and come here seeking information, which she refuses to give them. No one can know the truth. If they did, I fear what the council would do."

"If being born in Lupei is what creates the curse, then…"

It seemed so obvious to Liv, but she didn't know how to finish her question, feeling like she was being rude.

"We haven't always thought of being werewolves as a curse," Fane offered. "It was intended to be when the magician cast the spell, but over time, we took great pride in the fact that we were from the only place in the world where pure werewolves roamed, not these half-breeds who had been turned by those who left our town. My father's and mother's family were proud of our heritage, and I was too. Nicoleta and I wanted our daughter to share who we were. And because of your mother, we were sure she'd be safe to grow up in this world.

"For centuries, before the Bulgarians invaded our border, we'd lived peacefully, raising our livestock and feasting on that, never harming humans. Every few years, one of our own would grow restless and leave, spreading werewolfism around the world. However, that was a rarity.

"Recently, though, there was a shift in pack order. Our long-time alpha Relia died, and since then, everything has gone to hell. The new alpha isn't content with surviving the way we always have. That was when tourism started in Lupei, and the bloodbath quickly began. What happens at the inn isn't something that most of us here condone. We want to be separate from it, but we're powerless against the current alpha."

"You mean Soren?" Liv asked.

Fane cocked his head to the side, obviously not expecting that question. "Soren? Oh no, he isn't our alpha. Vera is. She was the one who killed Relia and took over the village. She's tired of us living under the radar, but she doesn't understand what we stand to lose. It was her sons who ran off and started the Bulgarian pack. That family doesn't get it. They want violence and blood, and they don't care who gets hurt or if we have to pay the price for it. They don't understand that killing innocent people is wrong."

"Wow...Vera," Liv said, having trouble believing that the old woman behind the desk was the mastermind of everything. "And the pack members who do what she says in the inn..."

Fane nodded. "They approve of Vera's ways, although the rest of us keep to ourselves."

"Not Papa, though," Alina said, bringing over a steaming bowl of stew. "He goes out at night and tries to stop them."

Liv took the stew, enjoying the savory aromas.

"I try, but it's no good," Fane stated. "They are too strong, and won't listen to reason. Every night is a different bloodbath with innocent people at the center of it. Vera has her men sell their stuff outside our borders and uses the money to advertise more about Lupei, ensuring that more tourists show up every single day."

"That's sick," Liv said, suddenly not wanting to eat.

Alina delivered a bowl of stew to her father. He took it, groaning deeply as he took a seat. "Can I trust you, like I trusted your mother?"

Liv took the piece of the crusty bread Alina offered her with a polite nod. "Yes, of course, you can. I know all too well what would happen if they learned the truth."

"But they'll want the names of the alpha and pack members," Fane stated.

"Yes, and you just have to tell me who those other men were in the tavern who were working with Soren," Liv stated.

Fane's face turned dark. "Not all of them are bad. Soren is, for sure. He's been wanting someone like Vera to take over for ages so he could run the show. However, many of the men don't have a choice. An alpha like Vera has a way of spreading influence. She makes threats until she gets her way. Before, when Relia was in power, things were peaceful. Those men were never a problem. Everything comes down to the alpha, and although I've tried to fight it for a long time, it will only be a matter of time before she has us all doing her bidding."

Alina sat down with a small cup of stew by her father's

feet and looked up at him. "You aren't like them, Papa. You can resist the alpha's call."

Fane dunked his bread in his stew and shook his head. "Not for much longer, my sweet Alina. Once the alpha exerts her dominance, I'll be powerless to resist it."

"Then every active werewolf in this village would be murdering tourists, wouldn't they?" Liv asked.

Fane chewed, his eyes sliding to the side. "It's worse than that. Vera has the power to draw the dormant wolf out. She could demand that our children turn at times other than the full moon."

Liv shivered. Werewolf children mauling innocent mortals? That was by far one of the sickest things she'd heard.

"Can you leave here? Get as far away from Vera as possible?" she asked.

Fane looked at his daughter. "I can't. For one, I'm bound to this alpha whether I like it or not. Her power over me is too great. Some have broken away, but the wolf is strong within me. Also, I can't abandon my village or those elderly in the general store. Or Claudia. They need me, and they can't up and leave."

Liv nodded, understanding at once. "I'll craft a plan to tell the council just enough information, then I'll return and help you take down Vera."

Fane's eyes glowed for a moment, nearly making Liv drop her bread into her stew. His gaze flew to the high windows. The sun had almost set.

He stood, setting his food on the counter in the kitchen. "I have to go out."

"You're shifting," Liv guessed.

He nodded. "I'm not a danger to you. I can control myself. All werewolves can. Most just don't want to. However, you'll need to stay inside with Alina. No matter what you hear, do not leave this house until morning."

Fane pointed to the cane sitting next to Liv. "No matter what, don't let that weapon out of your sight. It is the only silver in this village, and your only hope of surviving should one of Vera's break in here tonight."

CHAPTER SEVENTEEN

Once Fane left, Liv commenced pacing. There was no television to distract her, and no phone she could use to call Clark. No way to quell the anxiety building inside her.

After Alina excused herself to get ready for bed, Plato materialized beside Liv. She started, nearly screaming due to the tension bounding out of her chest.

"Where have you been?" she whisper-yelled.

He glanced around, taking in the humble dwelling. "It's not that easy for me to be here. There's something unnatural about this place, and it keeps trying to force me out."

"That's because everyone here is a werewolf," she whispered. Yes, Fane's secret was safe with her. She wouldn't even tell Clark, fearing that he might be bound to disclose the information to the council due to his oath. However, Plato was different. He was part of her, in a way, and she had to tell someone.

Plato nodded. "That makes more sense now. What

doesn't make sense, though, is why you're in a village full of werewolves at night."

"My magic is locked, and someone stole my cell phone," Liv explained. "I can't leave until morning, and even then…" Her voice trailed away, eyes widening with excitement. "Hey, can you go see Clark? Tell him to activate my magic. Tell him I'm okay, but I need to get out of here."

Plato's eyes closed for a half beat. "I'm sorry, but only you can request your magic to be activated."

Liv deflated. "Well, can you at least tell him I'm not dead?"

Plato sighed. "That's really not how I work, but…"

Liv flashed him a murderous glare.

"Yes, fine. I'll tell him you're okay," Plato said at once. "But my question is, *are* you okay? There are werewolves everywhere, and I can't stay much longer. The little girl is about to return, and she's one of them. I can't be in the same room with her."

"The rivalry between dogs and cats is never over, is it?"

"Something like that," Plato answered.

"Please just tell Clark that I'll call tomorrow, although I don't know how to reach him without my cell phone with all its numbers," Liv stated. "My money is all in my bag, which the dumb dogs took, so I don't even know how to get myself anywhere once I'm out of this village."

"Just get to the city," Plato offered. "I'll meet you there with Clark's contact information."

The door to the bathroom opened, and Alina appeared a few seconds later, a cautious look on her face. She was wearing a plaid nightgown, and her hair was pulled back from her face. "Who were you talking to?"

Liv looked around, grateful that Plato had disappeared. "Myself."

The little girl picked up the book she had been reading before and curled up in front of the fire. She patted the floor next to her, looking up at Liv. "Will you sit with me? I'll read to you from my book. That will help distract you."

Liv was about to ask "from what?" when howls cut through the night air, sending a shiver down her back. She tensed all over, her eyes darting to the door, which was thankfully securely locked.

Again Alina patted the floor. "Come. Sit with me. The pack will be up all night. Just try to ignore them. I'll read to you until you fall asleep."

Liv didn't know what to say. This little girl, much like Sophia, had had to grow up fast in a strange world. She knelt beside her, leaning against a pair of cushions and forcing a smile to her face. "Thank you," she stated.

Alina's eyes landed on the cane that Liv had left lying beside the couch. "Remember what Papa said."

Liv reached for the cane, pulling it to her side.

Alina nodded and opened the book. "Don't worry, they won't get in here tonight. But just in case."

Liv held the cane close to her chest as the girl started to read and the sounds of screams filled the air in the village of Lupei.

CHAPTER EIGHTEEN

Not until Fane returned the next morning and gave Liv the all-clear did she set off for the hills. She could feel him stalking her from a safe distance, which made her feel slightly better. However, seeing him fresh after his night as a werewolf was jarring. He'd arrived at his home battered and bruised. When she had asked him if he was all right, Alina had cut in, stating he'd be fine by the afternoon.

After a long and strenuous hike, Liv met the farmer, Palin. He didn't make any conversation as he drove her to the nearest city. When she got out, he sped away before she could thank him.

All Liv wanted was her magic unlocked so she could return home and try to figure out how to deal with the werewolves, and more specifically Vera, the woman who had turned a perfectly peaceful village of werewolves into monsters. It filled Liv with a sense of pride that she was working a case that not long ago, her mother had worked. She had never thought her life would parallel her mother's this closely. At times she felt like they were living in parallel dimensions, crossing paths, but only on the quantum level.

Liv had a lot of time to think about all of this, since when she finally got hold of Clark, he informed her that Adler was absent, and therefore they couldn't activate her magic.

"I can't stay in Romania," she complained, keeping her voice down so the shop owner who had allowed her to make the international call didn't hear.

"I don't know when Adler will return," Clark stated. "It's not like him to just disappear like this."

"But don't you have a meeting with the Seven tonight?"

Clark was silent for a long few seconds. "He won't be here."

"What?" Liv groaned. "I have to get home."

"I realize that," Clark stated. "I've bought you a plane ticket, and I'm wiring you some money. I've also pulled some strings so that identification shouldn't be a problem. You'll be home tomorrow, and Adler will have returned by then. That's when we'll unlock your magic."

"Can't you portal here and get me?" Liv asked, suddenly feeling very high-maintenance.

"I can't," Clark said regretfully. "We're knee-deep in sorting through information on the elf negotiations."

Suddenly Liv wished she hadn't sent Stefan away.

"Don't worry," Clark consoled her. "We'll get you home, and then everything will be okay."

No, it wouldn't be, because she was going to murder Adler Sinclair for this, and then have to face the council's wrath.

Liv gritted her teeth, thinking that the timing of Adler's long-needed vacation day was very strange. She then pictured the albino sitting on a beach in a Hawaiian shirt, lathering tons of sunscreen on as he read a cozy mystery. It was a visual that took away her appetite, although she hadn't been nearly as hungry as usual since not having her magic.

Thankfully, Alina had sent her with fresh bread and a bundle of dried fruit and nuts that had tided her over after the long hike. The little girl had also given Liv some money she'd pulled from a tin can they kept in the back of the cupboard. Liv left some of it for the shop owner who had allowed her to use his phone and left without a word for the airport.

"Do you know how many lines I stood in?" Liv asked Clark when he met her at the entrance to the House of Seven.

"I'm guessing more than one," he replied a bit sheepishly.

"Have you ever been to an airport?" Liv asked him as they strode down the long hall.

"No, but I hear they are fascinating places for people-watching."

"That's true, because guess what's everywhere?" She paused, but he didn't answer her rhetorical question. "People! They are ambling around without a clue where they were going, chatting on their cell phones like we all want to know what they are doing this weekend and not parenting their offspring, who, much like them, are glued to some device but not using headphones so that everyone gets to hear their music as they fail time and time again to beat a level of *Angry Birds.*"

"What's *Angry Birds?*" Clark asked, his brow furrowing.

"I can't help but think that you somehow missed the point of my story," Liv said with a tired sigh. She was still wearing the same clothes she'd had on in Lupei since she would rather have her magic unlocked than take a shower at that point.

"Well, speaking of devices," Clark stated, withdrawing a phone from his pocket, "I went ahead and got you a new cell phone. You think it was one of the pack members who stole yours?"

Liv nodded, averting her eyes from her brother's. She didn't want to lie to him, but the reality was that she was going to have to lie to everyone in order to protect the village of Lupei. She'd tell him the truth at some point, but not yet. He didn't need any extra stress. Her mother had confided the information to her father and he'd worked to help her, but apparently, that had put him in a dangerous position too. Clark had enough to deal with.

As if sensing her thoughts, Clark pointed to the cane that thankfully the security at the airport had thought was only a cane. "Did Father's weapon come in handy?"

Liv tightened her grip on it. "Yes, I'd say it's probably why I'm standing here right now."

Worry spread across Clark's face. "Well, hold on to it a little longer; at least until you've moved off this werewolf case. You might need it again."

"Is the beach bum back from his travels?" Liv asked when they paused outside the Chamber of the Tree.

Clark shot her a look of confusion. "Who?"

"Adler," she stated. "I'm ready to have my magic back."

"Oh, yes," Clark said, comprehension dawning. "He's here. Just arrived."

"I wonder where he had to go that was so important while I was stuck without magic in the middle of were-wolf-infested Romania," Liv complained.

"I don't know," Clark mused. "Honestly, I'm not sure he even left the House of Seven. No one saw him come or go. But it was strange for him to take a leave of absence, even for a day, and especially with everything we have going on."

Liv's eyes automatically slid to the Black Void. She could have sworn she heard whispering coming from that area, but she reasoned that it could also be the lack of sleep and airplane food making her hallucinate.

"Okay, well let's get into the Chamber," Liv stated. "I need a shower and a plate of nachos."

Clark agreed. "Yeah, you do need a shower. Sorry, but you smell sort of like a farm."

CHAPTER NINETEEN

Everyone in the Chamber turned when Liv stepped through the Door of Reflection. She couldn't help but notice that Stefan's face brightened with relief at the sight of her. Adler, on the other hand, didn't appear happy to see that she'd returned safely.

"Ms. Beaufont, was it really necessary to have your brother escort you into the House of Seven?" Adler asked when she took her spot.

Aside from Stefan, the only other Warriors in attendance were Akio and Trudy, who stood stoically, their hands behind their backs.

"Well, since I ran out of money for my Uber and someone had to pay the driver, yes, it *was* necessary," Liv stated. "Of course, I wouldn't have had to take a flight from Romania with two layovers and then a car from the airport if I'd had my magic." Liv tapped her finger to her chin like she was thinking. "Now, why again didn't I have my magic when stuck in Romania? Was it because you, Councilor DeVries, were away on holiday?"

Hester smirked at her playfully.

"Or was it because Councilor Ludwig had a stomach bug, and was stuck in bed for the last two days?" Liv pretended to ask.

Raina winked at Liv.

"Oh, that's right! I believe it was because strangely, you, Mr. Sinclair, had other business to attend to," Liv stated.

Adler's nostrils flared as he sat back, not at all looking impressed. "I assure you there was nothing strange about the timing. I simply had important affairs that couldn't wait."

"Right," Liv said. "A timeshare presentation you were obligated to sit through? Jury duty? Did you sign up to referee Little League football yet again?"

"Ms. Beaufont," Adler snapped, his irritation palpable. "What I was doing is none of your business, nor the council's. They are well aware of that, and you'd do well to remember your place."

"I would be greatly irritated too," Haro stated from his spot on the other side of the bench. "If I were stuck in Romania without magic and had to take mortal transport to return, I'd be making similar statements to you, Adler."

Raina nodded. "I agree. The timing of your departure was unfortunate, and although we all know that you couldn't avoid whatever it was that you had to do, Warrior Beaufont did have to suffer for it."

Liv smiled inwardly. The council was starting to rebel against Adler. Even if it was only in these small ways, it was progress.

"I will remind you all that Ms. Beaufont stated that she'd be out of Lupei by nightfall, and that was when her magic would need to be turned back on," Adler explained, heat flaring in his voice. "She did not phone us at that time, which was when I was available."

"That was because I had my cellphone stolen and found myself stuck in that lovely village," Liv stated. "Which, by the way, doesn't have wifi or cell phones, or even a freaking typewriter I could have used to write a message and send it to you by Pony Express."

"You are here now," Adler countered. "Did you find out who the pack members and their leader are?"

"I did," Liv answered. "However, I'm much better at telling this story with my magic. Will you all please unlock it? Then I can cast a perfume spell so I don't have to smell myself anymore." She gave Stefan a sideways look. "I smell like sheep and wet dog."

He nodded. "I'm afraid I know that already."

"I'm ready to unlock Warrior Beaufont's magic," Hester stated, turning a knob on the control panel in front of her. The other Councilors all murmured in agreement.

"Get ready, Ms. Beaufont," Adler said. "On my mark, Councilors. One, two, three. Go."

Whatever the Councilors did next, Liv didn't see. Instead, her vision was streaked with bright lights, and she felt a strange sensation surge through her chest. She nearly stumbled back like she had last time, but she was able to remain standing, remembering what Plato had said about breathing when having her magic unlocked. She inhaled deeply and flexed her fingers, feeling the power she'd missed for nearly three days flow through her.

To test her magic, Liv pointed at herself, freshening her clothes and body and getting rid of the farm smell.

"Much better," Stefan said, letting out air like he'd been holding his breath.

"Hey!" Liv complained. "I never get onto you when you show up smelling like demons."

"You probably should," he countered, flashing her a smile. "If we can't rely on our friends to tell us these things, we're doomed."

"You're right," she stated. "You have spinach or something in your teeth."

He didn't, but watching him pick at his teeth for the next several minutes was going to be entertaining. The crow flew down from an unseen place, cawing at her.

Stefan winked. "You're lying."

Liv stuck her tongue out at the bird. "Why did you have to ruin everything?"

"Diabolos has no concern for your affairs," Lorenzo stated. "He simply responds to lies."

Liv cut her eyes at the bird. She needed to shoo him away before she gave her speech—or maybe it was better that she'd attracted his attention with a small lie. Then the council wouldn't notice when she fudged the next few bits.

"Diabolos is his name?" Liv asked, glancing sideways at Stefan. "I would have taken him more for a Felix."

Stefan had his eyes pinned to the ceiling like he was trying to calculate quadratic equations in his head. Liv knew he was actually trying to keep himself in check in the presence of the crow.

"Your report, Ms. Beaufont," Adler stated dryly.

She nodded. "Yes, I'd love nothing more than to give that."

Diabolos cawed again.

Liv narrowed her eyes at the crow. "Seriously, you'd be a real downer at a garden party where everyone is supposed to make polite conversation."

"It isn't customary to talk directly to the Regulators," Bianca said with an admonishing glare.

Regulators, Liv pondered.

"And yet there aren't any laws against it," Liv argued. "I figure if no one gives them any attention, they are probably quite lonely."

"Your report?" Adler repeated, sounding even more irritated than before.

"Yes, so I've determined who the pack members and their leader are," Liv said, careful how she stated her information so as to not set off Diabolos.

"All of them?" Haro asked.

"Yes," Liv affirmed, careful to keep her eyes off the crow.

"Good," Adler stated. "Then you'll need to return to the village of Lupei and dispose of all of them."

"All of them?" Liv questioned. "I believe the alpha is the problem. There might be a few other loyal followers, but for the most part, they are simply men who have been forced to do their leaders' bidding."

"Although I know that taking out ten werewolves will be challenging, that's what has to be done to eradicate this problem," Adler said simply. "These werewolves know what the agreement states, and they are in direct violation."

Fane was right, Liv realized. If the council was aware that the entire village of Lupei was full of werewolves who were the only ones who could spread the curse, they'd probably vote for them to be eradicated too.

"I can help Warrior Beaufont," Trudy stated at once.

Liv wanted to protest, but she didn't know how to do so without drawing unwanted attention to herself.

Adler sighed. "Okay, very well. The two of you should be able to handle a pack of wolves. I want this problem dealt with swiftly. And if you're unable to take out all of the wolves, then Decar, you will be called in to take over."

"That won't be necessary," Liv said on the heels of his statement. "I'm certain that Warrior DeVries and I are more than capable of the task."

Her eyes fell on Diabolos, grateful that the bird was keeping its beak closed for once. Liv already had many doubts about returning to Lupei and fighting Vera while also protecting the innocent people of the village. Doing it with Trudy in tow was going to complicate things even further.

CHAPTER TWENTY

"When I move out, you'll be able to rent the place for tons more," Liv said to John as they stood on the long veranda she'd magicked, expanding her small apartment. The studio, which had been four hundred square feet, was now more than double that with a separate bedroom from the living area and a walk-in closet. Actually, it was no longer a studio apartment but a one-bedroom.

"You're not planning on moving out any time soon, I hope?" John asked, looking out at the street below from the roomy balcony. Jasmine flowers snaked their way through the arbors overhead, shading them from the sun. Before she'd spelled it, the area had simply been a fire escape with hardly enough room for one person, but now Liv had a place to drink her morning coffee and read the newspaper. She'd even joked to Plato that she could put a litter box out there for him, and he'd scowled in response. He'd never used a litter box before. Honestly, Liv didn't know where he did his business. More of the mysteries of the lynx.

"No, of course not." Liv looked at her handiwork appreciatively. "I just made the place the way I like it. I still don't know why you won't allow me to upgrade your apartment."

John waved her off. "I like my place the way it is. The upgrades to the shop were nice, though. Thanks to you, the place is perfect for all the new business we're getting."

"It was Clark who did all that," Liv admitted. "But thanks to him, I know how to expand spaces. At least, I'm getting better at it."

John looked down at where they were standing, worry springing to his face. "It's safe to be on this balcony, right?"

Liv didn't hide her apprehension. She'd tried several times to upgrade the floors, but the old one with the original cracked hardwood kept resurfacing after a few days. "You know what? Maybe we should go inside. I have a few more upgrades to make, then let's go out for pizza and donuts."

"Which one?" John asked, following her inside.

"Both," Liv chirped. "Why should we have to choose?"

"Well, I'm not sure my doctor would agree with that," John reasoned. "But I'm not a magician who can eat whatever I like, either."

Liv paused once they were inside. "On second thought, let's go to that new vegan restaurant down the street. I hear their hummus tacos are pretty okay."

John grimaced. "Hey, I don't want to die anytime soon, but that doesn't mean I have to force myself to eat rabbit food. Life is meant to be enjoyed."

Liv considered him for a moment. "Have you been taking your meds?"

He nodded.

"And drinking that superfood blend I got for you?" she grilled.

He nodded again.

"Fine, let's go for pizza, but we're getting mostly veggies on it," she stated, swirling her hand at the ceiling, making it go up several yards. "That's better. I needed a high ceiling."

"Wow," John said, marveling at the newly raised ceiling. "Do you think Ms. Goodwin above you felt that?"

"That senile old woman wouldn't notice if a spaceship landed in her apartment," Liv reasoned.

"This is really amazing magic," John stated. "I never saw Chloe use hers for anything like this."

"Oh, yeah?" Liv asked. "What did she use it for?"

John scratched his head. "I'm not entirely sure. A lot of potions. Conveniences. Sometimes she spelled people, making them do as she wanted. But her magic didn't feel as pure as yours, if that makes sense."

Liv nodded. This was the second time that John had mentioned feeling magic. That was an odd thing for a mortal to say, and not only because they'd been spelled not to see magic. John not only could see it, but he could feel it, which was similar to Rory. The giant was well acquainted with magic, being able to feel a magician's power.

"Well, I'm glad to have mostly mastered the expansion spells," Liv said with a sigh. She looked around and tried to decide what else she needed. That made her think of Mortimer, for some reason, and she decided to add a few windows to the place.

"That window is on an interior wall," John stated. "The

one that you share with my apartment. What exactly will the view be?"

Liv thought for a moment and then pointed at the window. "Well, why not have an ocean view? This *is* LA."

John took a peek out the window, marveling at the sight of the waves of the Pacific ocean rolling onto the beach below. "Wow. If I ever do rent your apartment, I've got some explaining to do."

"Seriously, John, let me upgrade your place with a gourmet kitchen or a movie room."

"Maybe..." he said, seeming to warm to the idea. "But not right now. I'm sure there are way better things you could be spending your energy on."

Like killing werewolves, Liv thought. She and Trudy would have gone to Lupei right after receiving their assignment from the council, since Liv didn't want any more innocent tourists dying. However, that was the night of the full moon, which would be the worst time to go there, knowing what she knew about the residents.

Trudy had wondered why it mattered, since the pack could change every night. However, Liv made up an excuse that they were more powerful on the full moon. It might be the truth, for all she knew, but what was certain was that being in a village of four hundred who were all werewolves was definitely not a good idea, and it would make keeping the truth from Trudy impossible.

She'd have to plan their trip carefully so that Trudy didn't see the elderly in the general store or learn anything else that made her suspicious. If everything went to plan, they would be in and out of Lupei before it got dark, having ended Vera's reign as pack leader.

"What I'd like to learn is how to create and throw fire-balls like a gnome with my magic," Liv said longingly.

John gave her an uncertain look. "I thought the gnomes were good at making cookies and crafting toys?"

Liv laughed. "Those are elves you're thinking of, the cartoon kind. Real elves mostly create artifacts that are imbued with magic. And they can be a pain in the ass if they catch you drinking out of a straw, which they state will pretty much destroy the Earth."

"Yes, they get stuck in sea-turtles noses, right?"

Liv nodded. "Something like that. But gnomes, who are a lot less sociable than elves, have fireball magic, which they've refused to share with me. They're also miners who have access to precious gems with magical powers."

"Well, I'm sure you'll wiggle your way into their good graces and learn their craft one way or another," John said good-naturedly.

Liv turned to appraise her work, thinking she was nearly done with the renovations. Then she noticed a small piece of paper floating down from the high ceiling. It landed on her new coffee table with a strange popping noise.

Unsure what this was or if it was safe to touch it, Liv took tentative steps toward the paper.

"What it is?" John asked, eyeing it.

"I'm not sure," Liv stated. "It could be a trap."

"It's a tiny piece of paper," he reasoned.

"I still can't trust it." She twirled her finger in the air, lifting the paper so it was even with her face. The sloppy handwriting said:

Liv Beaufont,

I've set up an appointment for your mortals to meet with Dr. Jay Dowling, the chief neuroscientist and genetic expert at UCLA.

Your friend,

Mortimer

Liv grabbed the paper, a smile springing to her face. "Hey, John. Are you up for a little excursion?"

He smiled, his eyes twinkling. "Of course. Whatever you'd like."

CHAPTER TWENTY-ONE

L iv pulled the stone from her cape that she'd gotten from Rudolf, running her forefinger and thumb over it.

"Rudolf, you Laffy Taffy, where are you?" she asked. She closed her eyes, aware that John was looking at her.

The fae appeared a second later with a popping noise, making her open her eyes. To her horror, he was wearing a kilt that showed way too much of his knees and thighs and no shirt.

"Well, hello, my lovely!" Rudolf said, throwing his arms wide. "Do you need a hug?"

Liv's gaze flew to John, giving him an uncertain look before glaring at Rudolf.

"I need you—"

Rudolf put his finger to Liv's lips, pausing her. "Shush. I don't need you to say another word. I knew this day was coming. Dear Liv, I know you're obsessed with me, but my heart belongs to another."

Liv slapped his hand away, rolling her eyes at him. "I

was trying to say that I need you to bring your mortal girl-toy to a doctor with John and me. I'm conducting an experiment."

Rudolf considered this for a moment, obviously thrown off his game. "So you want me to bring Serena to a place with your boyfriend so we can do a little two-on-two action?"

Liv tried as best she could to swallow the revulsion. "No, you jerk. John isn't my boyfriend, and there will be nothing gross between us. I want to take your girlfriend to a doctor to find out why she can't see magic but John can." Speaking slowly, like he didn't understand English, she said, "Do you know what I'm trying to say?"

He nodded slowly. "Okay, so you need me to go get Serena? What should we be wearing?"

"Well, first off, you need a shirt," Liv stated. "I really don't care otherwise, just cover your body. Maybe your face, too. Secondly, get her pronto, then we're off to UCLA."

Rudolf shrugged, looking half-defeated. "Fine. I'll go get her and return to you, but this sounds incredibly boring. Can we at least go to a club first? Maybe have a few Jell-O shots?"

Liv shook her head. "The appointment is in twenty minutes. Go get the train-wreck you brought back from the dead, then I'm throwing corpse-girl through an MRI. After that, you can go back to being totally annoying and draining society of its precious resources."

Rudolf bowed. "I look forward to nothing more."

After the fae disappeared, Liv turned to John with an

apologetic look. "Sorry, but I need his girl in order to create a test sample."

"No need to apologize," John said dismissively. "I think Rudolf is quite entertaining. I'm looking forward to meeting his lady."

"Actually, I think—"

"You little hooker, what do you want with my man?" Serena cut Liv off with a scowl, materializing in front of the Warrior with her arms crossed over her chest.

Unlike the first and only time that Liv had seen her, the mortal's face was full of color and her hair was styled, not plastered to her face from being submerged in a fountain. Liv gave Rudolf a disgusted glare after he stepped through the portal after Serena. Thankfully he'd put on a shirt, but he was still wearing the awful kilt that showed too much thigh.

Liv stuck out her hand, not at all deterred by the girl's terse insults. "Why, yes, you are quite welcome. It was my pleasure to rescue you from the bottom of a deep fountain that was protected by a deadly mermaid. You are so very welcome that I rescued you, thereby risking my very life so that you could have a second chance."

Serena threw her nose in the air, rejecting Liv's offered hand. "Ru, you're right. She's out for you. I see it now with my own eyes."

Liv nodded, having expected this. "By 'expected this,' did you mean that I needed you and Ru to accompany me to a doctor's office so that I can save all of the mortals from a crazy and dangerous spell?"

Serena shivered like she was suddenly cold. "I know what you mean now, Ru. She tries to pretend she isn't in love with you, making up reasons you should be together. I see the truth, though."

John stepped forward with an easy smile on his face, offered his hand to Serena, and knelt. "My dear mortal, do not worry about Liv. She isn't after your man. I assure you that he is of no interest to her."

"What does the strange man mean?" Serena asked Rudolf in a whisper.

"I think he's saying that Liv Beaufont is gay," Rudolf said in a stage-whisper. "That makes sense. It explains why she has shied away from me and my advances."

Serena shot him a heated glare.

"I meant before your heart was beating, of course," Rudolf added hastily. "I only ever fooled with other women when you were dead. And Liv wouldn't have any of it because of her sexual orientation."

"That isn't it," Liv stated indifferently. "I like men."

"When she says men, she means girls who are not you," Rudolf stated.

"I don't," Liv countered.

"And she's married to her job, and wouldn't notice a good man if he slapped her in the face."

"If he did, I'd put him in a headlock and ensure he could never father children," Liv remarked.

Rudolf chuckled. "You see what I mean, Serena? She's rough around the edges. Probably never going to attract a lover, whether she figures out her sexual orientation or not."

Liv sighed. "My sexual orientation, straight or not, is none of your business."

"Oh, magicians are always so limited, thinking they

must choose only one sexual orientation. Am I right?" Rudolf asked John.

Liv's friend didn't at all seem receptive to the question. Instead, he simply averted his eyes, looking to Liv to rescue him from the fae.

"Okay, we've got an appointment to get to, and I need you all to behave," Liv ordered.

"No problem, boss," John said, saluting.

Liv shook her head at him. "I'm not talking to you. I was referring to Rudolf and his corpse bride."

CHAPTER TWENTY-TWO

The foursome stepped through the portal outside the doctor's office. Although Dr. Jay Dowling was the leading expert in genetics and neuroscience in the country, Liv was unsure if this was even a viable option to find out about the mortals. She had no reason to believe there would be any differences between John's and Serena's brains based on the fact that he could see magic and she couldn't—although she was pretty certain that Serena's brain scan would come back showing that her head was full of rocks.

Thank goodness she's pretty, Liv thought, waiting for the mortal to step through the portal after John. She tripped after exiting the portal and would have fallen if she hadn't been holding Rudolf's hand.

"How did I get here?" she asked, spinning around and staring blankly at the area where the portal had been.

"You came through a portal," Liv explained, pointing. "Can you see it?"

Serena shook her head. "There's nothing there." She

turned to face Rudolf. "Is that vixen messing with me? Is there really something there?"

"I assure you that there is," John stated, answering for the fae.

Rudolf nodded, putting his arm around Serena's shoulder. "Liv Beaufont lies about many things, but in this case, she isn't."

"What are you talking about?" Liv asked, her tone full of offense.

Rudolf held up a finger. "You lied about your age, for starters."

"I've never lied about my age," Liv argued.

"Remember, you told me that you were only twenty-two, but you look so much older."

Liv let out a slow, deliberate breath.

Rudolf continued to tick off things using his fingers. "And then there are your lies about not having an obsession with me. Oh, and remember that time you lied to Queen Visa about giving her your blood?"

"So that she wouldn't kill me?" Liv shot back brightly.

"There's always an excuse for people like you," Rudolf stated. "And don't forget that time that you told that club full of people that you were Billie Idol?"

Liv rolled her eyes. "That was you."

"And I won't even go into the things that you've said while under oath," Rudolf continued.

Liv turned to John, giving him a sympathetic expression. "Jerkface has this problem where he projects his own lies and deceit onto other people. It's sort of adorable if you like horrible soulless people who have zero tact and suffer from delusions."

"It's very entertaining," John agreed with a smile.

Liv opened the door to the modern doctor's office. Since Dr. Dowling was an elf, she expected there to be incense burning and prayer flags hanging from the ceiling. Many of the elves she'd met were disgusting hippies who didn't work when Mercury was in retrograde or during the summer equinox or on the day of their monthly bath.

Authoritatively, Liv pointed to a set of chairs, ordering the group to take a seat while she checked them in at the front desk.

"The doctor will be right with you," the secretary said once Liv had written down their names and magically filled out John's and Serena's paperwork. Thankfully she was a mortal and didn't ask any questions about the quick turnaround. Knowing that answers were important, Liv was going to have to confide in Dr. Dowling, but she had a plan for how to deal with him afterward. She knew that too many people having the information would lead to her funeral. That was why she wasn't taking any chances.

When Liv took a seat, Serena was scowling at her from the other side of the waiting room. Ignoring her, she pulled out *Mysterious Creatures*, taking the opportunity to read up more on werewolves or whatever other chapter the strange book served up.

The book surprisingly fell open to a page on fae. It read:

The fae, although they appear as dense as pound cake and just as ill-equipped to deal with life's challenges due to their superficial nature, are an incredibly adept race that is better suited for surviving harsh conditions than most. They are fairly difficult to kill due to their genetic structure, which can amend to heal them when injured or cure them if they happen to contract a disease.

Liv peered over her book at Rudolf, who had his feet propped up on the coffee table beside him and was reading a children's book upside-down. Serena's head was lying in his lap and she had a serious expression on her face as he read from the pages, his voice too loud, making many of the mortals in the waiting room shoot him annoyed expressions. As usual, he'd glamoured his wings so he blended in with the mortals. Well, aside from being drop-dead gorgeous and completely irritating.

"Although Teddy didn't want to go to bed when his mother told him to, he knew he had a big day coming up. So he put on his pajamas and—"

"Hey, Dumbface," Liv said, cutting him off. "Keep it down over there."

Serena shot her a scathing look. "Would you not interrupt? We're in the middle of a pivotal part of the story."

"They all die," Liv said dryly, pulling *Mysterious Creatures* back up to read.

It figured that the fae were incredibly difficult to kill. Otherwise, Rudolf would have been dead a long, long time ago.

The fae do have some weaknesses that their adversaries can exploit in order to weaken them. However, the best defense against a fae is another fae. Whereas magicians and elves struggle to penetrate their tough exterior, another fae has little problem getting past these shields. It is for this reason that the fae rarely battle one another, knowing that the biggest weakness to their brand of magic is one of their own. The fae have little history of civil war because of this fact, knowing that if they turned on one another, they would be extinct in no time.

"The doctor will see you all now," the secretary said from the open door to the back rooms.

Liv rose, corralling the others and thinking of the strange information she'd just read. What was even more peculiar to her was that the book had served up that particular chapter. Rory said it gave the reader what they needed to know about at that specific moment. Did the book know that Liv wanted to kill Rudolf? Sadly, it seemed that battling him to the death would be extremely difficult.

Ironically, Liv and Rudolf were escorted to a cramped office while John and Serena had their MRI scans. She would have been content to sit quietly, continuing to read *Mysterious Creatures*. However, Rudolf apparently despised quiet, and promptly summoned a paddle ball and began knocking the thing around, sending the ball on its rubber band dangerously close to her. It was like the universe was trying to tempt Liv to kill the fae.

"Do you mind?" she asked after he'd almost hit her a third time.

He shook his head. "Not at all."

Liv let out a sigh and turned a page, not having read it.

"What do you think the meaning of life is, Livy?" Rudolf asked with a bad attempt at giving her a nickname.

"Pain," she said at once. "We're all here to see how much of it we can endure and, in your case, it's how much you can cause others by way of continuous irritation."

He nodded like this made sense. "I agree. I think it's love too."

"After this, let's take you to an ear doctor," she suggested.

"I was thinking the same thing," he said, paddling the ball harder. "Ice cream would really cheer Serena up."

Liv lowered the book. "Seriously, are you drunk? On drugs? What's your deal today? I mean, more so than other days."

Rudolf stopped paddling. "Thanks so much for asking about my well-being. I do have something on my mind."

"That's not what is happening here," Liv stated.

As if he didn't hear her, Rudolf continued, "I'm thinking of asking Serena to marry me, but I'm nervous she'll say no."

"You brought her back from the dead."

"I know, but I worry that it wasn't enough," Rudolf said, leaning forward and placing his elbows on his knees.

"Ummm…you gave up a hundred years of your life for that hussy. I think you're good."

"So you think we should get married, then?" Rudolf asked.

"I absolutely don't give a damn either way."

Rudolf nodded. "I know. It must be awkward for you, with all your pent-up feelings for me."

"Nope. Not an issue. Just promise me you'll never breed."

"Speaking of which," Rudolf said with a smile. "If I do ask Serena to be my wife and she says yes by some miracle—"

"Again, without you, she'd be dead."

"Not everyone is like you, swayed by such small acts of

affection," Rudolf said with a huff. "Really, it's no wonder you don't have a man. You have to make them try harder."

"Wow, why haven't you opened up a counseling business?" Liv asked, with zero inflection.

"Anyway, as I was saying, if Serena accepts my proposal...well, I know this will be strange, but I was hoping that you'd be my best man at the ceremony."

Liv shook her head. "Nope. I can't. I'm busy that day."

Rudolf frowned. "We haven't set a date yet. She hasn't even said yes yet."

"She will, and it doesn't matter what the date or time is. I can't make it because you two getting married will make me want to vomit."

Rudolf nodded in understanding. "Jealousy is toxic. It *will* make you sick. But I can't get married without you by my side. You're my oldest friend."

Liv tilted her head and furrowed her brow. "We've only known each other for a couple of months."

"I know!" Rudolf exclaimed. "And yet, you're like the sister I never had. You're like one of my cousins, except that we've never slept together."

"Okay, I seriously need a barf bag," Liv said, covering her mouth from repulsion.

"So does that mean you'll do it?" Rudolf asked.

Liv shook her head. "No, but I'll send you a second-hand clock radio I repaired that gets horrible reception and only plays AM as a wedding present."

Rudolf beamed. "I absolutely adore you too. And don't worry, I won't tell Serena about that one time that you kissed me."

"Nope," Liv said at once. "That was you kissing me, and I punched you in the face."

Rudolf held his hands to his chest and gazed at her fondly. "I treasure that memory more than all the rest, too. Well, until we start vacationing together and spending every single holiday with each other."

"I. Cannot. Wait," Liv said as the nurse entered the room.

"The doctor is ready to see you all now," she stated.

Liv stood, hoping this trip hadn't entirely been a waste of time and brain cells.

CHAPTER TWENTY-THREE

Dr. Jay Dowling didn't look like any of the elves Liv had met so far. He resembled Santa Claus, with his white beard, bald head and round belly. However, he appeared quite serious, unlike Saint Nick, when she took a seat in front of his desk. She'd left John with the awful job of having to watch Rudolf and Serena while they read children's books and braided each other's hair in the waiting room.

The doctor tapped the stack of papers on his clean desk, looking at Liv uncertainly.

"Is there something you want to tell me about these two patients you had me scan?" he asked her.

Liv considered this question for a moment. "Yes. The first, John Carraway, can see magic, and the other one, Looney Tunes, cannot. I'm trying to determine if there is a physical difference between them."

He raised a bushy white eyebrow. "You say that John can see magic? And he's a mortal?"

"Yes, that's what I'm trying to figure out," Liv explained. "Like, is he a genetic anomaly? If so, what are the differences between someone like him and someone like Serena, who can't see magic."

Dr. Dowling nodded and put on his reading glasses. "That actually helps. Mortimer, who set up this appointment for you, didn't give me any information, so I was operating blindly, which I thought was maybe better so that I could be more objective."

Liv was relieved that Mortimer wasn't giving away any information. "Was there a significant difference between John's and Serena's brain scans?"

He opened the file, reviewing it. "There was quite a startling difference. Genetically speaking, John is definitely a mortal. However, I ran some other test using magic and his DNA structure is somewhat different from most."

"What does that mean?" Liv asked, leaning forward in her seat.

Dr. Dowling shook his head. "I'm not quite certain. It's strange, but I have reason to believe it has something to do with why his brain operates differently than Serena's."

"So these differences...do they pertain to magic?" Liv asked, her heart suddenly beating fast.

"Oh, yes," Dr. Dowling stated, peering at the files. "I'm not sure I ever would have caught this if you hadn't brought John in to see me. Now, after hearing what you've told me, I believe something is affecting the cognitive receptors related to magic in Serena's brain." He held up one of the scans and pointed to a highlighted area. "This is the part in the brain that you and I use when we create magic. That same area is where we also perceive it. As you can see from the scan, this area in Serena's brain is dormant, and has never been used, which I always believed to be typical for all mortals."

Liv was surprised that Serena had used *any* of her brain but didn't say anything, keeping her attention on the doctor.

He held up another scan. "This is John's, and as you can see, that area of his brain is used, but not to the extent that mine or yours or other magical creature's would be."

"Which is because he can see magic," Liv guessed.

Dr. Dowling nodded, putting the pages on the desk and combing his fingers through his beard. "The question I'm hypothesizing is, what is different in John's genetics that makes it so this area of his brain works?"

Liv grabbed the diagrams, studying them. "What if I told you that mortals all used to be able to see magic, just like John."

The surprise made Dr. Dowling's eyes widen. "That's quite startling."

"Does it mean the genetics of mortals has changed over time?" Liv asked.

He thought about this for a moment, then shook his head. "I don't think so. Not to this radical an extent. To me, it appears that John was born with an evolutionary quality to his brain that allows him to see magic. His ancestors probably had this and passed it along to him."

"Evolutionary quality?" Liv asked. She had always known that John was special, but not like this. And the bit about ancestors struck her oddly. What if the structure of the Mortal Seven was different from that of other mortals? She shook off the thought and focused.

"Now, if what you say about how mortals used to see magic is true, then the next question is, what is preventing people like Serena from witnessing it?" Dr. Dowling mused. He massaged his temples as he looked over more notes. "Honestly, I'm just going to make a guess after reading these files and say that it's possible there is something that is being broadcast that inhibits this part of mortals' brains from functioning properly. John's genetics make it so that this wouldn't work on him. Of course, this is all just a guess, but that's how science starts."

Liv cocked her head to the side. "Wait, like a transmitted signal? Is that possible?"

"Not only is it possible, but I've conducted extensive research on the subject," Dr. Dowling answered. "Mortals' brains are incredibly easy to effect with a signal broadcast from a specific location. I've hypothesized that someone could affect them globally if they so desired."

"Like if someone wanted them not to see magic?"

"Exactly," Dr. Dowling said triumphantly. "However, that signal wouldn't work on John, as evidenced by his scan."

"So this signal…how could we locate it?" Liv asked.

Dr. Dowling pondered this for a moment. "That's a tricky question. It would have to be magically broadcast. Only something with magic could have such far-reaching effects, which means it would have to be sent from a geographical location that holds a certain level of mystical power."

Something caught in Liv's throat, and she suddenly couldn't breathe. "Like a place with high elevation?"

Dr. Dowling nodded. "That would be the first important factor. Then it should also have a certain quality of wonder, like the Great Pyramid or Niagara Falls."

"What about the Matterhorn in the Swiss Alps?" Liv asked. "Would that be a significant enough place for brainwaves to be transmitted?"

"Oh, yes," Dr. Dowling said at once, suddenly excited. "That would be a prime location, and would protect the power used to broadcast and ensure it had reached the intended audience."

"So you think it's possible that someone is broadcasting a signal that inhibits that area of the brain, making it so mortals can't see magic?" Liv asked, needing to confirm this information.

"Yes, that's what all the information points to," Dr. Dowling said. "Although I would need to do more tests to determine the facts, and I plan to do so. This is a subject that needs all of my attention. I have many colleagues it will be of interest to as well."

"And John appears to not be affected by this because of the distinctive makeup of his brain?" Liv questioned.

Again Dr. Dowling nodded. "I'm sure it's possible there are other factors that would inhibit the transmitted signal. Maybe if the mortal was exposed to a pure source of magic or left Earth for an extended amount of time, or, well, there are a few scenarios I can think of which might work. However, genetics would be the most likely factor."

The canisters, Liv thought with a sudden burst of adrenaline. What if Adler had the rogue bits of magic put into the canisters and sent them away because if mortals were exposed to them, they could see magic again?

Liv stood, taking the files from Dr. Dowling's desk. "Thank you. This has been incredibly helpful."

"Those are actually my files," he stated, his lips curling in disapproval. "I'll need them to continue the research, but I'll have copies made for you."

"I know, but I have to take these," Liv said, gathering up the last of them. "I'm sorry, and I also apologize for what I must do now." She pointed her finger at him and muttered a quick incantation.

"What you must do?" Dr. Dowling asked, standing at once and shaking his head. "And you can't take those. They're my only copies. This is huge. Mortals seeing magic! Someone broadcasting a signal that inhibits others from seeing magic. A genetic anomaly. There is so much research to be done here. So many..." He looked around, bewilderment covering his face. The doctor shook his head like he'd just awoken from a strange dream.

Tentatively he extended his hand to Liv. "Hello. I'm Dr. Dowling. What can I do for you today?"

Liv offered him a small smile, hugging the files to her chest. "Actually, I was lost and just happened into your office. I'll be going now."

He nodded, looking around his desk like he'd misplaced something. "Very well."

Liv let herself out of his office, hurrying lest her presence spark any of the memories she'd erased from the doctor's mind. She didn't like tampering with his mind about their conversation or the tests he'd just run, but it had to be done. Now she had even more reason to visit the Matterhorn. Her parents had gone there for a reason, and maybe, just maybe, it was to turn off whatever was transmitting the signal, thus enabling most mortals to see magic again.

CHAPTER TWENTY-FOUR

Trudy DeVries looked like a warrior out of a history book when she stepped through the portal outside Lupei, Romania. She was wearing dragonhide armor, carrying a round shield, and holding a long sword.

In comparison, Liv looked like a homeless magician. She stared down at her solid black cape and her father's cane.

"So, although I think you look freaking fabulous," Liv began, peering at the small village below, "I think your outfit sort of screams, 'We've come here to kick your asses.'"

Trudy took the position beside Liv, her boxy jaw held high as she appraised the land. "That's generally the impression I was going for. What are you trying to communicate?" She gestured to Liv's modest clothes, which were enchanted to keep the bitter cold out.

"I'm going for an innocent look," she explained. "Something that says, 'Hey, I'm no big deal. You should probably underestimate me, up until the moment that I kill you.'"

Trudy nodded appreciatively. "I do not doubt you. I'll admit that your record so far is impressive, and I'd like to learn more about your untraditional approaches. Like, how did you and Stefan slaughter Sabatore, the Master Demon?"

"I strolled into a deserted courtyard and pretended to be a lost, dumb blonde to lure him out of his hiding place," Liv stated, remembering the awful smell when the disgusting demon had grabbed her.

"Oh, so you use this unsuspecting approach often then?"

"When it makes sense," Liv answered.

"Although I respect your input," Trudy countered, "we're going to slaughter a pack of werewolves, so I think first impressions are important."

Liv had respected Trudy from the beginning, even though she'd had little chance to interact with her. Unlike Decar Sinclair and Emilio Mantovani, she didn't have a smug, self-entitled glare constantly plastered on her face. And unlike Maria Rosario, she didn't walk around with an air of mystery.

Trudy, whether it was a good or bad thing in her role as Warrior, appeared to carry her emotions on her face. When Adler disciplined her, shame covered her features, and when she disagreed with something the Council said, it was plainly written in her hazel eyes.

Liv had worked with Hester, Trudy's sister, and knew that the council member and healer could be trusted. She was keeping Stefan's secret about being bitten by Sabatore, and she'd kept Liv's secret about being bitten by both a mermaid and a lophos. However, it was wrong to believe that just because she could trust one family member, she could trust another. From a logical standpoint, it made perfect sense. Family stuck together, and they thought in similar ways. They were usually loyal to the same causes.

And Liv knew, from Stefan that Trudy was sympathetic to the unregistered magicians she'd been forced to round up based on the council's decree. For that reason, she was going to take a chance with the Warrior.

"I don't think we should take out the entire pack," Liv began, carefully watching Trudy's face for signs of resistance.

"Because?" she asked.

The easy answer was because taking out the entire pack would mean slaughtering an entire village. That was too big a secret to spill, however, even if she thought she could totally trust Trudy. Not only that, it was a burden. Sometimes offering people information wasn't giving them power. It was making them shoulder an unnecessary load they'd be forced to carry alone.

Liv knew what that was like as she stared down at the seemingly idyllic village below, and even the most well-meaning magician might see this secret regarding Lupei as a huge problem. Wipe them out, and the werewolf epidemic would be gone—no more unnecessary murders related to werewolves who had gone mad. Bermuda had said in *Mysterious Creatures* that werewolves were unpredictable and deranged, even without the full moon. Although others had soiled their reputation, Liv had looked into Fane's eyes and known he was different. His people were different. They were disciplined and could control the werewolf.

"The pack leader, Vera," Liv began, "has a hold on a couple of members. Maybe only one. We'll have to figure that out. However, most of the others are innocent men who have been forced to do her bidding. Under different leadership, they might act differently."

"But they may not," Trudy countered.

"Adler informally leads the council," Liv proposed. "Do you think Hester should be punished if he suddenly started making them do things they didn't want to do?"

"Suddenly?" Trudy asked with a laugh.

So she wasn't completely blind to his influence. That was something.

"The law states that when a pack gets out of hand, they're to be punished," Trudy recited.

"Yes, but what if the law is wrong?" Liv countered. "What if a pack follows its leader, no matter what? Those who created those laws hadn't spent any time with were-wolves. They didn't know that the pack is at the alpha's mercy. Whatever she orders them to do, that becomes law. They can't go against it, even if they want to."

"Much like us," Trudy mused.

Liv shook her head. "No, very much unlike us. We aren't governed by pack order. We have free choice. Which means, we have the ability to do what we think is right regardless of what the law states."

"So what are you proposing?" Trudy asked.

"I think we need to take out Vera and her second in command," Liv stated. "Then we reconvene and see how the pack changes. If they are still a problem, we take out the rest of them."

Trudy gave her a reluctant expression. "I've never done things this way."

"You mean where you go against the council's orders?" Liv questioned.

"No, I've done that more often than I care to admit," she answered. "In our role, I think it's difficult to always follow everything the council wants. They totally don't get it. In the field, people are different than how they appear in the case files. But I've never chanced leaving a potential problem out there."

"What about when you've allowed unregistered magicians to go?" Liv argued.

"That's different," Trudy rebutted. "Those are our own kind. They might be led astray. I've tried to get them to do the right thing, and I've followed up with them, giving them several warnings before doing as the council stated."

Liv shivered, thinking of Trudy killing magicians just because they weren't registered with some overbearing government agency. She knew the Warrior had a good heart, but she wasn't accustomed to thinking for herself. It was hard to be objective when the council was supposed to think for you.

"Werewolves are people too," Liv began. "So are giants and trolls and gnomes."

"Right, and fae as well," Trudy added.

Liv lowered her chin. "Barely. Don't take it too far."

Trudy laughed.

"My point is that we've taken to seeing them all as separate. You'll show compassion for our own kind, bending the law for them. However, others don't get that same leniency."

"And you think they should?"

"I think that if we're doing our job as Warriors, we have to take each case as it comes," Liv stated. "I'm not saying we should disregard the law. More like we use it as a flexible blueprint that we modify depending on the landscape and materials and whatever else plays a role."

Trudy considered this. "That was a good analogy."

Liv smiled. "Thanks. I tried not to take it too far. Otherwise, I might have lost my momentum."

Trudy snapped her fingers and her appearance shifted. The bulky armor and shield disappeared, and the sword was exchanged for a staff. She gave Liv a hopeful look. "Okay, let's try things your way. What's your plan?"

CHAPTER TWENTY-FIVE

"You really like being bait, don't you?" Trudy remarked after Liv told her the plan.

"Yes, apparently I have a death wish of sorts," she answered. "That's why I eat chili-cheese burritos, even knowing how they will make me feel later."

"I like how you live dangerously."

Liv flashed her a smile as she started down the hill. The plan wasn't complicated, but it did offer some flexibility, depending on how things went. And also it wasn't Liv and Trudy charging forward, blindly massacring werewolves without first offering them a chance at salvation.

"I'll meet you in an hour," Trudy called after her, standing tall on the high hill.

The werewolves in the village would know that a magician was approaching. They'd feel her magic, about like how giants did. That was why timing had to be crucial. Liv placed a speed spell on herself, making it so she moved like a werewolf, stealthily and so fast her legs felt as though they'd come after her.

Thankfully she was still acquainted with the layout of the village, since it made it easier to negotiate. Liv sped by the bus of tourists before they stopped outside the inn. She would have preferred to portal into the town, but wards prevented that, which was typical. Every place except her apartment and the electronic shop seemed to have protections like that. It was probably overdue that she placed them around those areas, giving up convenience for security.

The door to the inn was still swinging from her entrance when she came to an abrupt halt in front of Vera, who, as before, was standing behind the counter.

She glared at Liv, her nostrils flaring. "I should have seen you for what you were, magician."

Liv took note of the werewolves crowding in from the tavern, Soren in the lead. "You may call me Warrior, pack leader."

"You have some gall coming into my town alone," Vera spat, her gray eyes flicking to the pack at Liv's back. "Did you find out what you needed when you came in on your first visit?"

"I know that you're in direct violation of the agreement with the House of Seven," Liv stated, feeling the hairs on her arms rise.

Dark veins had started to radiate from around Vera's eyes, making her look like she might shift at any moment. It wasn't nighttime, though.

The werewolves could only change then, Liv told herself. But then she remembered the elderly in the general store. They were stuck like that. What if Vera *could* change? She was older for a werewolf, probably the oldest in the immediate pack. Liv hadn't counted on them fighting shifted werewolves. This was supposed to be a quick and easy fight.

"Supposed to." Those dreaded words that echoed in her brain just before everything went wrong.

The tiny movement of Vera's eyes should have gone unnoticed by Liv, but the speed enhancement spell she'd placed on herself made it so she didn't miss it. She knew that if she was going to fight werewolves, she needed to have reflexes to match theirs.

Soren had rocked back on his heels, about to spring forward when Liv flicked her hand over her shoulder like she was shooing a fly away. Soren flew back into two other pack members, all of them smashing into the wall.

Without taking her eyes off Vera, Liv leaned down. "How about we discuss this matter privately? Otherwise, I fear we'll keep getting pesky interruptions."

Vera didn't at first appear willing to indulge Liv on this request. However, Liv knew the only way it would work was to separate the alpha from her pack. The men would lay down their lives to protect her, which meant they'd all die.

"Soren," Vera said, a growl in her throat. "Take this intruder to the back."

Liv shook her head. "Although that sounds lovely and not at all like a trap, I'd prefer the wide-open space of the inn. So, what you're going to do is have your pack go outside and tell all the tourists who are clogging up the street to get back on the bus. Then the driver is going to take them out of this town, giving them some excuse they'll believe. Starting today, no more tourists will die here."

Vera's eyes began to glow as the veins darkened, spreading to her cheeks.

"When your men are out of here," Liv continued, "you and I are going to sit down like reasonable people and discuss the agreement with the House of Seven and how you can avoid violating it again."

Cracking her neck to the side, Vera narrowed her eyes. "That doesn't sound like a good deal to me. And you may have a bit of magic, but you're nothing up against all of us."

"That's true, but you don't want to get in trouble with the House of Seven for harming one of their beloved Warriors, do you?" Liv dared to ask, although she already knew the answer.

"I don't give a shit what the House of Seven thinks," Vera said with a sneer.

"Let the tourists leave, and then we'll discuss this," Liv requested again, buying them the much needed time.

Vera shook her head, her long gray hair swaying. "My boys are hungry. *I'm* hungry. Those tourists are ours."

"I sort of figured you'd feel that way about the perfectly reasonable arrangement I offered," Liv stated matter-of-factly.

The sound of the bus's engine firing up made Vera's ears twitch. "What did you do, Warrior?"

"Since I figured you wouldn't be at all compliant, I took it upon myself to go ahead and run the tourists out of town," Liv said, working to keep her voice even as Vera's eyes glowed hotter. "Apparently, those tourists think the inn had been shut down due to a pest infestation." Liv tapped her chin like she was thinking. "I have no idea where they got that idea."

The roar of the bus speeding out of town brought the men at Liv's back closer. She could feel them breathing down her neck, but she didn't dare give them her attention.

Liv had done her homework on this one. She knew all the power resided in the old lady standing in front of her. If the men were angry, it was only because they shared a connection with the alpha. She told them how to feel, and what to do, and when to do it. They were her robots, forced to do whatever she wanted. Fane and the others in the village were somewhat removed from her direct line of control, but they were still a part of the pack. A second tier, as Liv had come to think of them.

"Warrior, you'll pay for this," Vera snarled, lifting her chin and looking at the men behind Liv. "Go and try to get them back. Soren, you stay with me. We're going to give this young magician what she wants."

So far, everything was going to plan. Fane would be waiting for the men, and he'd do his best to keep them away, but hopefully not pay too high a price to do it. That was why Liv had to be fast. The longer they spent in Lupei, the greater the risk that innocent people would be injured.

"Good," Liv said as Soren sidled up next to her and the other men filed out the door. "You're going to find a way to work within the agreement. I knew you would be reasonable."

Vera shook her head. "Oh, no. I would rather die than do that. It might have been good enough for my ancestors, but eating sheep when we were meant to prey on humans is not my way. You wouldn't understand."

"So what do you mean, you're going to give me what I want?" Liv asked, confused.

Soren smacked his fist in his palm, leering down at her. "We're going to give you a fair fight, Sally. That's what you want, isn't it?"

Liv looked between Vera and Soren, feeling suddenly tiny. "How is this a fair fight? There are two of you and only one of me?"

"We all know that magicians are stronger than were-wolves when we haven't turned," Vera said, coming around from behind the counter. She was so plain in her jeans and button-up flannel that it was odd to think she was the pack's leader. "So, two on one. That's the fair way."

Liv rolled her eyes; she had expected all this. Not only had Bermuda's book filled in many of the gaps, but Alina had also advised her the night she had stayed in Lupei.

"Now, first of all, we need to get that pesky cane away from her," Soren stated, his breath smelling like rotten meat as he exhaled on Liv.

"I'd give it to you, but I need it to walk," Liv joked. "Well, if you really want it, I guess I can give it over." She handed him the silver, but he shied away like the sight burned him.

Soren went for Liv's other side, the one opposite the cane, but the door at the front burst open. Standing on the threshold in a long traveling cloak was a shadowy figure.

"One of the tourists," Vera said in a hushed voice to Soren. "Bring them in here."

Trudy pushed back her hood to show her short, spiky hair and smoldering hazel eyes. The staff she'd been carrying before materialized in her hand as she stepped forward into the light.

"I'm no tourist, but I would like to come in," she said, a blast of green light radiating from her staff and knocking Soren into the back wall. He collided with a bookcase, cracking all the shelves as he slid to the ground.

"*Two* Warriors," Vera said, her words hot with anger.

"Oops," Liv said. "Did I forget to tell you that I brought a friend? My bad."

Trudy came to stand next to Liv, both of them regarding Vera with mild contempt.

"You have one last chance to surrender and do things as the council dictates," Liv ordered. "If you don't, then we'll have no choice but to put you down."

If Vera was intimidated by being outnumbered and her best mutt having been subdued, she hid it well. Actually, she must have thought Liv was a comedian because she began to laugh.

Trudy looked sideways at Liv, probably wondering if she was wrong and this was not the alpha, just a looney old woman.

"Do you know how I defeated the last alpha?" Vera asked, leaning forward, her back hunched slightly.

"A really boring game of chess?" Liv guessed.

Vera shook her head, sidestepping like a wolf circling its prey. "My family is the only one with magician blood to ever be born in Lupei. Not only does the wolf live deep in my bones, but the same magic that flows through you runs in my veins."

Oh, hell! Werewolf magician. Liv hadn't been expecting that.

"Not the same," Liv said. "We aren't corrupt, and neither are the others in your pack. You're power-hungry, and you have let it go to your head."

Vera shook her head, hunching over more. "I've finally come into my own. It took me a long time to get control over my magic after keeping it a secret for all of my life. My family never wanted anyone to know. They wanted us to live in the shadows, just like everyone in this town. But I knew there was a better way. My way."

She sprang from the floor, hands extended, and grabbed the rickety chandelier overhead. Swinging her legs, the old woman flew to the other side of the room and landed with a thud, one hand on the floor and the other in the air. Soren followed a similar path as her, flying through the air as if he were suspended on hidden wires.

Using her magic, Vera dropped him by the door, where he stumbled upright, appearing as though he'd just awoken from a gnarly nap.

"You know, this inn has been in my family for a long, long time," Vera said, her voice gravelly.

Liv was just about to plan an attack when she realized that her arms were pinned to her side. She jerked her gaze to Trudy and read the same frantic expression on her face.

"This inn is special to us," Vera continued. "And therefore it has certain charms that work only for us. It does our bidding."

Liv tried to break free from the invisible restraints that bound her arms to her side, but she was unable to do so.

"I do look forward to dealing with you both soon," Vera said, her eyes sliding to different places around the room.

"However, let's reconvene later. Say, after sunset—when I've changed into something more comfortable."

Vera then grabbed Soren by the arm and yanked him outside, shutting the door to the inn behind them and locking Liv and Trudy inside.

CHAPTER TWENTY-SIX

As soon as the door shut, the immobility spell was gone, allowing the Warriors to move again.

Chewing her lip, Liv turned around slowly to face Trudy. "Soooo…"

Trudy closed her eyes for a half-beat to calm herself.

"That bit about her being a magician was new," Liv said, glancing around the inn, trying to figure out how they could possibly escape.

"Which makes her a hybrid, and not someone I want to face after dark when she's shifted," Trudy stated.

"My thoughts exactly, which means we've got to find a way out of here." Liv pointed to a vase on a high shelf, trying to determine if it was a magical artifact that Vera had used to seal the place shut.

"I suspect that if what Vera says is true about the inn, there is no easy way out unless she releases us herself," Trudy said, trying the door and finding it sealed shut, not just locked like a regular door that would budge a tiny bit.

This one was magically sealed in place, no air even coming through the cracks.

"There has to be something that Dogbrain missed," Liv said, picking up a slight magical vibration from the vase. "Vera looked around at certain places before darting out of here. Do you think that the place is sealed using artifacts?"

"I think it's possible," Trudy said, pulling out her cell phone and then frowning.

"Let me guess, no reception?" Liv asked.

"Yes, which is odd, since I've been able to call out both when I was three hundred feet underground and a mile in the air."

Liv arched an eyebrow at the Warrior. "I think I need to hear the stories regarding those locations."

Trudy cracked a smile. "Well, it appears that we'll have several hours to exchange stories. You can tell me how you got that bite on your leg and the other one on your arm."

Liv froze. Her bites were covered.

Hester had told Trudy! That was the only explanation. Suddenly Liv felt shortsighted for trusting the Councilor.

"Do you know how Hester is a healer?" Trudy asked her, partially hiding a smirk.

And a liar who doesn't keep her word, Liv thought. Instead of saying that, she simply nodded.

"Well, in our family, each member is gifted with a strange and rare ability that doesn't pull from the magical reserves," Trudy explained. "I know it's weird, and after I tell you this, you don't have to shield yourself. It wouldn't do you any good anyway."

Liv tilted her head to the side, wondering what the hell the Warrior was going to say next.

"I have x-ray vision," Trudy admitted. "I try not to use it, but it's sort of automatic. Most of the time I don't even know I'm doing it, but it's hard to ignore that huge bite on your leg or the one on your arm."

Liv looked down at her covered limbs. "So you can see…"

"That you're concealing a sword under your cape," Trudy stated. "And also that you're wearing mismatched socks."

Liv sighed. "Is nothing sacred anymore?"

Trudy chuckled. "It's a weird gift. Usually it doesn't give me the advantages most would think. Actually, most of the time, it makes me sympathetic to my enemy. It's hard to take them seriously when they are wearing Batman underwear."

"So can you only see through clothes?" Liv asked. "And if so, that's the creepiest gift I've ever heard of."

Trudy pulled a pair of glasses from her cape, sliding them on. They were tinted greenish-blue. "I had a friend make these for me. They prevent my gift from working. If you'd like, I'll wear them when I'm around you now that you know the truth."

"So the council doesn't know?" Liv asked. "They know about Hester, though, don't they?"

"Yes, but that's because Hester's gift is important and has saved many a Warrior," Trudy began. "Mine can be practical in battle, but there's no real reason for me to disclose it. Our parents were sensitive about our gifts, not wanting us to be exploited for them."

"Yes, I could see how you'd be targeted if people knew."

"And to answer your question," Trudy continued, "I can

see through almost anything, within reason. Not too thick of walls or from really long distances, but if I'm close to something, I can usually make out what's on the other side."

"That's incredibly valuable," Liv stated. "Is there anyone else in the inn? Anything you see that might help us?"

Trudy pulled off the glasses, searching the space before shaking her head. "No, we're alone in here. And I'm not certain. I have my doubts about getting out of here. I've tried to find a weak space with my magic, and the building is locked up thoroughly."

Liv nodded, having tried the same thing.

Trudy slipped the glasses back on and strode past Liv in the direction of the tavern. "Well, it sounds like we need to strategize for when that door is open and Vera has changed."

"Where are you going?" Liv asked, following her.

"I don't know about you," Trudy called over her shoulder, "but we're going to need food to keep up our reserves, and I could use a drink. Maybe while I'm fixing us something, you can tell me what took a hunk out of your leg and why my sister didn't tell me about it?"

"How do you know that Hester knows anything about it?" Liv asked.

Trudy stopped, giving her a skeptical expression. "Does she?"

Liv wanted to lie, but Trudy's eyes seemed to cut right through her. "Yeah, maybe."

"I thought so." Trudy continued into the tavern, headed for the kitchen. "If I was mauled by something like whatever attacked you, I'd call my sister too."

CHAPTER TWENTY-SEVEN

"I just wish you'd make more potatoes," Liv said, ladling a heaping pile of the mashed potatoes which were overflowing from a large pot onto her plate.

"Ha-ha," Trudy stated. "I told you the other vegetables weren't really up to my standards. And the meat? Well, it looked questionable."

"Please tell me it wasn't human," Liv said, pushing her plate away, suddenly not hungry.

Trudy shook her head. "No, but it definitely wasn't fresh. I'm guessing that they don't keep anything fresh on hand since they catch theirs every day."

Liv took a big spoonful of potatoes and eyed the lumpy mess. "Were you hoping that if Vera defeats us, we'll have the last laugh when she realizes you boiled every single one of her potatoes?"

Pointing with her fork at the pan, Trudy chewed with her mouth slightly open. "I'm hoping if you help me finish that pot of mashed potatoes, Vera won't be defeating us. All we need is a good plan and our reserves full."

"She'll be changed, though," Liv argued, staring down at the blob of white on her plate.

"There are two of us."

"But she's part magician," Liv countered.

"You've got that cane," Trudy said, taking a sip of her whiskey. Liv had declined any alcohol, thinking it was better to keep her head clear. The other Warrior had said she actually thought better after a single drink.

"And she's got a pack of seemingly loyal pups."

Trudy smiled between bites. "We'd make a fine good cop, bad cop pair."

"I'm guessing that means I'd be the bad cop, doesn't it?"

Trudy nodded. "You have some valid points, and that's why we have to be strategic. If I was betting, I'd guess that Vera will be less about strategy and more about simple assault. That's why when she lets us out of here, we have to do something unexpected."

Liv thought for a moment. "What if we set fire to the place? Werewolves hate fire, right?"

"That's vampires," Trudy corrected. "But everyone hates fire. Well, not demons. I think they eat it. However, I fear we'd die from smoke inhalation. This place is sealed up tight."

"Maybe we set up a series of traps inside here? When she walks in, she'll fall into a pit of blades."

This gave Trudy pause. "I like that idea, but honestly, I think we have to get out of this place as soon as she opens the door. The inn has too many advantages for Vera, and we have no idea where the pack is. We don't want to be ambushed in here."

Liv agreed. "The entire pack will have shifted. It will be hard to determine which one is Vera."

Trudy smiled. "For that, you can rely on me. I know exactly how to tell which one she is."

"Oh does that x-ray thing work for that?"

She nodded and took another sip.

The two fell silent for a long minute while they thought, the wheels turning in their heads.

"So, the bite on your leg?" Trudy asked after a long bit.

"I fell," Liv said simply.

"Yes, and Stefan fell too," she said with a wink. "Don't worry, I'm not going to pry if you don't want to tell me. I get having your own life and missions outside of the House."

Trudy stretched and stood, letting out a long groan. She was built more like a man, with her broad shoulders and narrow waist. "I'm going to go use the little girl's room. Be sure to fill your reserves, but don't worry about doing the dishes. I think we can leave them for someone else to clean."

Liv smiled, swirling her spoon in the potatoes and making a design.

As soon as Trudy was gone, Plato materialized on the table beside the pot of food.

"How do you know when the coast is clear to appear?" Liv asked him.

"It's a gift," he said simply.

"Like x-ray vision?" Liv asked.

"No, more like the ability to pick the lottery numbers, which I can do as well."

"Oh, really?" Liv asked. "I've been so poor I couldn't buy

us dinner, and you know how to pick lottery numbers? Why didn't you ever tell me?"

"You wouldn't want to be handed anything," Plato told her smugly.

"Try me."

"So, you're stuck in an inn surrounded by werewolves, and the sun is less than an hour from setting," Plato mused, sounding rather amused.

"It's going to make quite the story to tell at dinner parties," Liv stated.

"Unless you become dinner tonight." Plato licked his paw. "Then I guess I'll be the one telling the story."

"Be sure to include that I tried to take you down with me," Liv added.

"But like the coward I am, I ran before the pack could get me, leaving you defenseless and alone."

"Yes, be sure to include that part."

Plato shook his head. "I don't think so. It doesn't paint me in the best light. But if it helps, you'll know the truth."

"Okay, well, then just be sure to say a few nice words at my funeral, would you?"

"You know I can't do that," he answered.

"I know that you *won't*," she corrected.

"And before we order the stale croissants and flower arrangements for your service—"

"I don't want flowers at my funeral," Liv cut in. "You know I'm allergic to most of those things. Instead, I want balloons. And everyone must take a hit of the helium before they say nice words about me, or whatever they say."

"I've made an update to the affair," Plato stated. "However, don't get ready for the Big Sleep just yet."

"Do you have a way to get us out of this inn?" Liv asked, hope flocking to her voice.

"No. I can pop in and out, but you're absolutely stuck here." He looked around. "Whatever Vera's family did to this place, they made it vault-like. You're not getting out of here until she takes off the charm. Your friends have been trying for a while to get in through the back, but it's no use."

Liv smiled inwardly, proud that Fane and Alina were still trying to help her. He must have been very fond of her parents. How could anyone not be?

"Did you have an idea that might help us?" Liv asked. "Something to delay our deaths?"

"Yes, I think I do," he stated proudly. "I'm hoping that it does more than postpone your death by several hundred years. If it works, you'll reset the balance of this entire village, thereby reinstating peace among werewolves."

CHAPTER TWENTY-EIGHT

"Are you sure this is going to work?" Trudy asked from the first landing on the stairs, looking down at Liv dubiously.

"No, not at all, but it's the best plan we have," she answered.

"And how do you know that Soren is perched on the roof?"

"Call it a hunch," Liv said a bit sheepishly.

Trudy gave her a hesitant expression. "And the rest of the pack? How do you know they are located around the perimeter at the back?"

"Wild guess."

"Okay, fine," Trudy stated. "Keep your secrets. If you weren't so cute, I probably wouldn't go for this whole thing."

"Isn't that bad logic to base your decision-making on?" Liv asked her.

Trudy shrugged. "Probably, but I also like it when you make Adler angry. No one has been willing to be as bold as you in…well, for as long as I can remember. Even your mother didn't dare to say the things you do to him, so I guess I'll trust your judgment purely out of respect."

Liv smiled. "I think that's as good a reason as any."

Continuing the climb to the second story, Trudy shot Liv one last look. "Be careful. And if you need help, you know what to do, right?"

"Scream like bloody hell?"

"That's right," Trudy said, disappearing around the corner.

Liv held her father's cane in her hand, hoping that Plato was right about the placement of all the pack members in the village of Lupei. One mistake, and she and Trudy would be dead. The plan was to divide and conquer. A pack of werewolves was impossible for a single Warrior to defeat, but one was manageable. However, Liv knew she wasn't facing just any werewolf. She was about to face off with one of the deadliest to ever exist.

Although Trudy DeVries knew Liv Beaufont was hiding something, it didn't worry her. Everyone was concealing a part of themselves. Sometimes that was because it was easier that way, or because they didn't think they'd be accepted if others knew the truth about them. That was Trudy's reason for not telling others who she really was. Trudy might have been able to see under people's clothes, but that wasn't her biggest secret.

However, Trudy suspected that Liv had different reasons for keeping secrets. For some reason, Trudy thought Liv was hiding something bigger than the House of Seven, but that was only a guess. And whatever it was, Trudy was okay with Liv doing whatever she was doing. There was a competence in the young magician that inspired trust. Trudy and Hester had discussed it many times. Liv Beaufont, as mysterious as she was, seemed to be straightforward. What you saw was what you got. She was fighting for only one thing, whether her agenda was apparent or not: the greater good.

When Trudy came to the third-floor landing, she marched to the far end, as Liv had told her to do. The sun would be down in less than a minute, which didn't give her as much time as she'd like to set up for the next part.

Blinking at the closest wall, Trudy activated her x-ray vision to see through it. At first, she couldn't see much past the roof, but then the small figures on the ground around the building materialized. She counted six. That was how many Liv had said would be on the ground, ready to storm in through the back.

How the girl had known the werewolves would be stationed there, Trudy couldn't fathom, but she had been right. They were exactly where she said they'd be. And it made sense that they'd enter through the back, or be there if Trudy and Liv tried to escape that way.

"Okay, now it's time to find number two." Trudy scanned the area around the upper floor until she found a figure standing just on the other side of a window blocked by shutters. "Bingo."

Soren stood only a few feet away, still in human form. It was almost time, but not quite. Trudy knew what she'd have to do when Vera opened the inn. However, she'd have to be fast. Timing was key. And she hoped that if she was successful, it would mean that Liv was too. Leaving the young magician to do what had to be done hadn't been easy. And yet, she knew she had to. Liv was the right person to face the alpha. If anyone could take her down, it was Guinevere's daughter.

CHAPTER TWENTY-NINE

L iv tried to tell herself that she'd been in worse situations as she stared at the sealed front door, but the truth was she couldn't think of a direr one. Yes, she'd been caught by Sabatore and nearly been kissed by the demon, but she'd had faith that Stefan would step in and save her. She'd been bitten by the lophos and nearly died, but even then she'd trusted the people around her to help, and Clark had come to her rescue.

But this...

Liv knew that when she faced Vera, she would be absolutely alone. Trudy's job was to handle the rest of the pack, which was quite the job for one person. All Liv had to do was take down a single werewolf...who had magic. No biggie.

The lights flickered overhead, and the inn shook. Howls echoed around the building.

It was definitely party time, Liv thought, yanking her cane apart to reveal the two swords.

The chandelier's bulbs extinguished, leaving Liv in total darkness.

"I see she wants to make a grand entrance," Liv muttered to herself, placing a night-vision spell on herself. The room illuminated enough that she could make out the door again. It shook, and then the large wooden slab flew off the hinges and soared in Liv's direction. She dove at the last minute, rolling out of its path.

Crouching, Liv spun to face the doorway and realized she was frozen yet again. The devilish woman had placed another immobility spell on her, but thankfully it wouldn't last long.

According to Plato, a werewolf couldn't do magic when shifted. He suspected that as a werewolf hybrid, she'd be stronger and deadlier than any other due to the magic, but she couldn't cast any spells. That meant she'd had to take down the wards barricading Liv in the inn before shifting.

Liv realized once she looked out the open doorway that Plato was absolutely correct. The unassuming old woman's body contorted oddly as she began to shift. The sounds of bones cracking and fabric tearing made Liv flinch. This should have been Liv's chance to blast the not-fully-transformed werewolf and escape from the confines of the inn, but she couldn't move. Instead, she was forced to watch the painful transition, unable to do anything she'd planned.

It took less than a minute for the small woman to transform, then standing squarely on the threshold was the stuff of nightmares. Sabatore had nothing on Vera in werewolf form.

The monster was covered in thick gray hair. Her long snout dripped disgusting drool, and her narrow eyes glowed red. Vera stood on her hind legs, her front ones covered bearing long claws that she held in front of her scarred chest. This was not a dog that was going to win any contests. No, she was so large that she had to duck to enter the building.

When the lights went out in the inn, Trudy could still see just fine thanks to her x-ray vision. It had been why she was never afraid of the dark when she was younger.

The floor shook under her feet.

So far the place was still locked up tight and the werewolves hadn't shifted, but she had a feeling that everything was going to change over the next several seconds.

Multiple times, Trudy tried to break through the window in front of her using her magic, but they were still trapped. That only made the werewolf shifting on the rooftop in front of her, just a few feet away, even more chilling. The process appeared incredibly unnatural as the beast's bones contorted at weird angles and it grew taller.

Scanning the area, Trudy noticed the other six figures shifting. A chill ran down her spine at the vision of the many werewolves taking form. Trudy had always loved animals, which made what she was going to have to do next even more difficult.

She reminded herself that her empathy had gotten her in trouble with the council more than once. However, Liv shared this same affliction, and it had served her in many different ways.

Trudy had battled inside about the right course of

action here, but had finally concluded that Liv was right. It was possible that not all the werewolves had to die. Yes, that might be the right option. If the alpha and her second in command were in fact the problem, why punish everyone?

Trudy knew what it was like to conform. She'd been doing it all her life. If Liv was right and the other werewolves were punished for doing things they couldn't control, she wouldn't be able to live with herself—and the last thing that Trudy DeVries needed was more guilt.

A loud crash on the first floor made Trudy spin around. Something had happened below. She couldn't see to the first floor from the third, but her magic told her exactly what she needed to know.

The spell had been lifted. They were free to leave the inn, which meant the werewolves were also free to enter.

A growl that made Liv's ears ache escaped the werewolf's mouth. It held its head up to the ceiling, its long arms extended like it was trying to hug the night for setting it free.

Liv's fingers twitched around the cane. The immobility spell was wearing off. Vera had placed it on her right before shifting, but it wouldn't last now that she'd changed. Any second now, Liv would be able to move. As soon as she could, she'd need to get the hell out of that place.

The werewolf slammed down on its front paws and growled at Liv, who was only ten feet away. Too close.

The hot air spilling from Vera's mouth soared across

the space, making it feel like a furnace had suddenly been turned up. The beast's breath was putrid as it accosted Liv in the face.

She threw up her arm to shield her nose and was grateful to find she could move once more. Vera, however, wasn't as happy about it. She lunged, but Liv darted to the side fast enough to avoid being tackled. The werewolf collided with the front desk, making the thick wood buckle. She was like a bulldozer, strong and crushing.

As Vera worked to untangle her large form from the broken pieces of the desk, Liv shot a stunning spell at the werewolf, but it did nothing.

Liv's magic didn't work on Vera. It must have been a protection placed on her as a hybrid, which meant that Liv might be absolutely screwed.

Without magic, she had to rely on the only two things she had to her advantage: her intelligence, and her father's cane.

Holding up her hand, Trudy sent a powerful stream of magic through the large window in front of her, blowing it out of its frame. It flew several dozen feet, landing on the roof of a building across the lane.

The sound of the breaking glass got all of the dogs' attention, which gave Trudy the perfect opportunity to soar through the open window. She landed with a thud in front of Soren in werewolf form. If he had been ugly before, with his wide nose and small eyes, then he was even more repulsive now that he was covered in fur.

He whipped his head over his shoulder, his bright green eyes landing on Trudy. Before he had a chance to growl or react or whatever, she held up her staff, wrapping his body in an electrifying spell. It made his limbs stretch out as he was rocked by the internal shocks. As Liv and Trudy had suspected, Soren not being a hybrid made him susceptible to magic, giving the Warrior a fighting chance.

The pack at her back was moving in closer and Trudy directed her attention to them, creating a line of fire using her staff. It cut the six werewolves off from the inn, making them shield their faces from the sudden burst of flames. Carefully using the staff her grandmother had given her, Trudy raised the flames until they were high above the werewolves, too tall for them to jump.

An angry, deep growl resonated through the night air behind Trudy. She knew what doing the fire spell had cost her. It had released Soren from electrocution.

She turned to face the werewolf, delighting in the fact that his fur was still steaming. However, crouched, he still appeared strong enough to do a lot of damage. And unfortunately for her, she had to make a choice. Keep the fire wall up, barricading the werewolves away from the inn, or take out Soren?

Trudy held her staff horizontally, ready to use it as her grandmother had taught her. The woman's words echoed in her head. "When you can't rely on magic, use brute force. One day you'll be a Warrior who fights for magic but ironically doesn't get to use it in all situations."

CHAPTER THIRTY

Sidestepping in the direction of the entrance, Liv tried to not make a single noise. Vera was still yanking her claws free of the splintered wood.

The inn was going to need a major renovation after this fight.

A piece of the wood from the broken door cracked under Liv's boot and she froze.

Vera brought her large snout around to find Liv standing only a few feet from the entrance. She considered making a break for it, but the way the werewolf moved made Liv certain that she wouldn't make it off the porch before she was tackled.

No, I must keep my eyes on the beast. Turning her back on Vera was a recipe for death.

"Hey, little puppy," Liv said, holding the silver swords in her hands and taking a fighting stance. "Would you like to play fetch?"

Vera jerked loose of the broken wood, landing with a thud that made dust rain down from overhead.

Akio had taught Liv to use the dual swords together in a way that could cause a distraction. He called it sword illusions, and many soldiers used it in battle to hypnotize their enemies, confusing them until they could get a clear shot. He called it a last resort because it was apparently what someone did when they had limited options left. That was definitely Liv right then.

Bringing the blades of her father's cane over her head, Liv alternated bringing them around at lightning speed, blurring them through the air. The blades made gentle clanging noises as they met and parted several times on different diagonals.

The werewolf swayed slightly, her paw shuffling to the side to catch her when she was close to falling over. That awoke her from the daze, and she grabbed a piece of broken wood in her jaws and slung it in Liv's direction. It rocketed at her so fast that she didn't have time to deflect it. Instead, it slammed into her right shoulder, knocking her into the wall. The sword in her right hand clattered to the ground, rolling under debris from the front desk.

Liv held tight to the remaining sword as Vera took a step in her direction, her eyes glowing hot.

Soren balanced on the uneven surface of the roof with ease. As he took a step forward, the roof groaned under his weight, sagging slightly.

If Trudy had thought of it, she'd have put a weak spot in front of him, making him fall through. That gave her an idea, though.

Without warning, the werewolf launched himself at Trudy, his long claws reaching for her. She brought the staff across his head, knocking him to the roof. As big as he was, she wasn't dwarfed by him, thanks to her own formidable size.

Looking over her shoulder, Trudy checked to ensure that the werewolves were still being kept at bay by the fire. Most of them prowled around the perimeter looking for an opening. However, a couple had disappeared. They might have figured out they could go around the village and get through on the other side. Either way, it was still worth keeping up the fire barrier. Liv couldn't deal with more than one werewolf while facing the alpha. Hopefully, once she was down, the spell would be broken and the pack would disperse until a new leader was chosen. Trudy didn't know how such things were decided. She guessed that the one who killed the alpha became the next one, but what if that was Liv? Could she be the leader of a werewolf pack? That would make her one badass Warrior. Well, more so than before.

Soren shook his massive head, dispelling the daze the blow from Trudy's staff had caused. Blood trickled from one of his ears, dripping through his fur.

She took her stance again, ready for another assault. Instead of running at her, he sprinted for the open window she'd come out of. Trudy realized a moment too late what he was doing. He was going after his alpha.

"No!" she yelled, making a quick decision. She sent a neat beam of light at him from her staff and it caught him on the tailbone, making him slam into the side of the window's frame and howl in pain. However, undeterred, he shook off the attack and crawled through the broken window, then limped down the hallway toward the stairs.

Trudy was about to take off after him when the bright light behind her disappeared. She spun to find the firewall had gone down, and the werewolves staring up at her with pure vengeance. She had to make a choice: keep these away from the inn, or go after Soren?

He's injured, she told herself as she worked to put the perimeter back up. As soon as it was strong enough, she'd go after Soren and help Liv.

She could sense that the werewolf was about to pounce. It was evident in every one of Vera's movements. She was biding her time, trying to figure out how to get the sword out of her hand. That was the only thing standing between the wolf and Liv, and they both knew it.

Liv pulled her hand back, holding the slender sword like a spear. She'd practiced enough with it to know that it had good flight characteristics, and could easily hit its target if needed. But if Vera moved fast, she could avoid the assault.

A loud clunking sound pulled Liv's and Vera's attention away from each other. Liv took a step away from the wall, straightening fully. She was expecting Trudy to materialize from where she'd gone up to the third floor. Things were about to shift. Trudy must have taken care of the other werewolves.

Two Warriors on one hybrid was much better odds, Liv thought.

A moment later Soren appeared in werewolf form on the first landing, his teeth bared at Liv.

Oh, hell. Two werewolves on one Warrior was much less favorable.

The alpha and Soren exchanged meaningful glances. Liv didn't speak werewolf, but she was certain they'd communicated. She held onto the sword and looked between the two, wondering what was going to happen next—and then it all became clear. Soren started forward, springing in Liv's direction.

Of course, the alpha would require that he sacrifice himself for her to get the sword from Liv. He ran at her, a furious force of muscle and power. When he was only six feet away, he sprang into the air, his jaws open and his teeth dripping drool.

Liv didn't think twice before launching her father's sword at the werewolf, the blade going straight into his chest. He grabbed, gasping and fell down to the floor in one swift movement. She had no time to react before a force like a tornado knocked her to the wooden floor, claws piercing into her shoulder. Liv tried to wrestle out of Vera's clutches, but the werewolf had her pinned.

She'd been tricked, but how could she have done it better? Her magic was useless on the werewolf, but maybe if she used it indirectly, she could free herself. Liv tried to summon her wind magic, but the fear pounding in her veins prevented her from doing anything but cringe as Vera's snout raised into the air and howled fiercely, victory coursing through the air.

The monster brought her mouth down, sniffing along

Liv's neck to find the sweet spot. Liv tried to move, but it was useless under the weight of the beast.

The werewolf growled low in her throat. At any moment she'd tear into Liv's flesh, and it would all be over. Still Liv didn't give up. She moved her hands around on the floor, trying to find the other sword. If she could just get it, then...

Something slammed into the werewolf on her, freeing Liv. She didn't take a second to look but rather rolled to the side until she hit Soren's dead body, which had returned to human form. Stumbling to her feet, Liv blinked at the sight in front of her. It was hard to tell what was happening as two beasts wrestled; hard to tell where the giant gray werewolf ended and the black one began.

Liv grabbed the sword from Soren's chest, yanking it free just as Trudy raced down the stairs.

"Here," Liv said, tossing the sword in her direction. She caught it gracefully.

Liv dove under the debris, grabbing the other sword as the two missing werewolves appeared at the front door.

"They went around, but the others are still barricaded," Trudy said. "You take the one on the right, and I'll take the one on the left."

Liv shook her head. "No, they don't want us." She pointed with her sword at the two werewolves wrestling. Vera had thrown Fane across the tavern. "They are here to stop that fight at their alpha's orders."

"Well, we can't have that," Trudy stated.

Liv agreed with a nod, holding up her hand. "Yes, this isn't really our fight. We might have started it, but the real alpha has to end it." As Vera had done before, Liv sealed the entrance to the inn, blocking the werewolves from entering. Now they were locked inside with two werewolves. That was either a great idea or the worst one ever.

The first werewolf charged, thumping into the invisible door and fell back. The other prowled back and forth, his eyes roaming as he looked for another way to get in there.

This fight couldn't last much longer. And by the looks of it, it wasn't going to.

Vera's teeth sank into Fane's side, making him howl in pain.

Liv tightened her hands on the sword, ready to run after Vera and end this. However, Trudy held up her hand, stopping Liv.

"You were right, this isn't our fight," she said in a whisper. "If you win this for him, he'll never have control over the pack."

"But if he loses…" Liv said, fear taking her over.

Trudy tapped her sword against Liv's and offered a rare smile. "Then we will have to finish the job ourselves."

Liv nodded as another howl rocketed through the air. This time, to her surprise, it was Vera. Fane had thrown her across the bar and she landed with a thud, bottles crashing down on her.

To her surprise, Fane limped away from the werewolf. Liv wanted to scream, "She's not dead!"

To her shock, Fane morphed into human form as he approached. It was like watching a strange pixelated movie, making Liv think she was losing her vision. Bleeding and looking more dead than alive—and mostly naked—he ripped off a piece of cloth from his ripped shirt and wrapped it around his hands several times. Then he extended his thick hand in Liv's direction.

She didn't know what he wanted at first, but then he combed his hands through the air and she understood.

Relinquishing her sword, she placed it in his hands. He nodded appreciatively, striding back in the direction of the bar.

"Let the pack in here," he yelled to Liv with an authority she couldn't argue with.

She brought down the wards and the two werewolves prowled into the inn, which was crumbling in places, the ceiling looking close to falling in. At their backs, the rest of the pack appeared. Liv pulled Bellator, ready to defend herself, but the werewolves didn't give her the slightest bit of attention. Instead, they sauntered into the tavern, growls emanating from their mouths.

Undeterred by this, Fane stood on the other side of the bar, his eyes narrowing on the pack as they came closer, all of them looking ready to attack. He shook his head at them.

Liv saw Vera's claws grip the other side of the bar. She was about to scream, "Watch out," but Trudy pressed into her, making her stay silent.

The other set of claws hooked into the bar. Gripped.

Fane's attention was solely on the pack, a whole host of information seemingly transpiring between him and them in long stares and growls.

Liv almost screamed when Vera sprang over the bar and straight overhead, flying in Fane's direction. For a second, she appeared to be suspended in the air. She was about to crash down on him, tackling him to the floor, but then as if he had simply been waiting for it, he spun around, rammed the sword through her chest, and shoved her back onto the bar.

Almost instantly, the large wolf shrank into the form of an old woman, the silver sword protruding from her chest. Blood covered her body.

He turned back to the pack as if he'd done nothing more than rid the tavern of a pest. He dusted off his hands, which were covered in blood, and shook his head. "What's done is done. We kill no more innocents from this point forward. Is that clear?"

In unison, every single werewolf in the tavern cowered, making whimpering sounds. And one by one they began to shift, turning back into the men they had been before Vera made them do horrible things.

CHAPTER THIRTY-ONE

When Trudy extinguished the fire, the residents of Lupei came out with wide eyes to meet the new alpha of the oldest pack of werewolves in the world. Their pack.

Liv didn't say a word, but instead walked beside Fane as he greeted each member of his pack one by one. Each bowed their head to him, and although he didn't say anything, she could feel the words he somehow expressed to them. *The werewolves must be telepathic,* she realized. Or at least the alpha was with the pack. It was beautiful to watch, actually, like they were all part of the sea and he was the wind, blowing each of them like waves across the ocean.

Trudy joined them when there was a break in the procession. "The fires are out. Should I help repair the tavern?"

Fane smiled but shook his head. "That won't be necessary. We'll be disassembling it and creating something new that we can be proud of." He turned to Liv. "If you'll excuse me, I need to speak to someone."

She nodded, watching as he disappeared into the crowd of people. It was well into the night, and yet the entire village was out, mingling and talking. Laughter could be heard everywhere. There was a celebration about to break out, Liv could feel it.

"You were right," Trudy said by her side, her hands clasped behind her back and her chin held high as she appraised the crowd. They were outsiders and were being treated as such, corralled to the outskirts of the festivities that were starting to take place in the center of the square. However, Liv knew why. No one wanted them to know the secret. No one knew that she knew it. And only two knew she'd never reveal it.

Liv rubbed her hand on her stomach, feeling it rumble. "You mean that you should have made more potatoes?"

Trudy laughed, then pulled a protein bar from her cape and handed it to Liv. "Here."

Liv took the bar with a grateful nod.

"And no," Trudy began, unwrapping her own protein bar. "You were right about not taking out the whole pack. Soren had to go. He was undoubtedly corrupt. However, those other men? I watched how they responded when Vera died. They were released. If we would have killed them…"

Liv turned to Trudy, listening to her as she eyed the protein bar. It smelled like sugar, which contrasted with the scent of roasted meats that was strong in the air as women paraded around with pans of food and carafes of beer. "The law says that the entire pack goes down when they break the rules. However, not everyone is responsible for what some members do. They shouldn't be punished for what one person does."

Trudy nodded slowly, something working behind her eyes. "How did you get so wise at such a young age? I must be double your age, and I don't know all this."

Liv thought for a moment and took a bite, her mouth turning up in a smile from the sensations the taste gave her. "Wow, what is this? It tastes just like…"

"Chocolate cookie dough," Trudy supplied. "Yes, I refuse to eat things that aren't sweet. I get all my calories from desserts."

Liv nodded appreciatively at the other Warrior.

"I can't carry a tray of brownies around with me, so these have to do," Trudy said, holding up her own protein bar.

"And I don't know," Liv began, trying to answer the question Trudy had asked her to begin with. "I constantly feel this ticking in my chest that reminds me of my parents' voices. It's my compass. Even when I don't know what to do, it seems to."

Trudy clapped her hand on Liv's back. "I don't know where you came from entirely, Liv Beaufont, but I'm sure glad you came out of that hole, wherever it was."

The two chewed on their protein bars, watching the festivities in the village with appreciation. "They are happy," Trudy finally observed.

"I think they finally have the chance to be, after a long time," Liv added.

"Do you mind if I leave you here?" Trudy said, rolling up her wrapper and sticking it in her pocket.

Liv did the same and nodded. "I think I can find my way home."

"Cool," Trudy said, stepping back toward the hills they'd come down. "And I don't know how you knew that the pack would be around the perimeter and Soren on the roof, but I'm glad you did."

Liv tapped her head and smiled. "Magic."

Trudy saluted her. "You are an enigma. I'd say I'd be keeping an eye on you, but I think I like you better with your secrets, Liv Beaufont."

Liv saluted back. "Thanks for your help, Trudy DeVries. I look forward to working with you again."

Trudy turned, waving with her back to Liv as she strode for the hills. "Until next time."

Liv watched her stride away until she was too hard to see.

"Does she know anything?" Fane asked by her side, having materialized out of nowhere.

Liv turned to him and shook her head. "Not a thing."

He smiled and was about to say something when Alina ran up holding a bouquet of flowers.

"These are for you," she said, thrusting the small white blossoms into her hands.

Liv knelt and took them from the young girl. "Thank you, Alina. These are beautiful."

"You saved our village, Warrior Beaufont," Alina said, hugging her. She was strong for a young girl and kind for a child who would grow up to be a werewolf.

Liv stood and stared at the man before her. "Oh, I didn't do anything. Your father saved you. He saved this entire village."

Fane's eyes fell to the cane in Liv's hands, and he nodded. "I couldn't have done it without you. And I intentionally used your father's cane to end Vera's reign so that the pack remembers their place. We aren't invincible and if we are going to prosper, then we must cooperate with magicians, not oppose them."

Liv hadn't thought of the implications of Fane using a sword to take down the alpha, but this made sense. And it had symbolism, which she liked even more.

"I hope you continue on your path, Liv Beaufont," Fane continued. "I fear you have many hardships ahead of you, but I hope you succeed. I hope somehow you avenge your parents' death."

Liv held tight to the cane in her hands, pulling it close to her chest. "Just like you, I'll die trying if I have to."

He cast his eyes over the village full of joyous residents. Somewhere in the general store, Claudia was caring for the elderly, hopefully telling them the worst had passed. The town of Lupei had gone through hell and come out the other side, and hopefully one day the House of Seven would be able to tell a similar story.

"I hope you don't die trying, but if you're anything like your parents, you won't give up until justice is served." He extended his hand, still bruised and bleeding, although it looked much better than it had an hour before. "And if you ever need anything, you know you have friends here."

Liv took his hand, shaking it with a great fondness for the man before her. The one who had given her father the sword that had saved her life that night.

CHAPTER THIRTY-TWO

Q ueen Visa had many things going for her. She was the most beautiful woman in the world, her powers were seemingly unmatched, and she was beyond patient. Being a fae and living for centuries allowed for such things.

For a very long time, she'd been planning to destroy a single place. Doing so had gotten extremely complicated when the magicians had increased security. She gripped the vial of blood in her hands, overjoyed that the day had finally come when she could destroy the House of Seven.

The council forced their laws on other magical races, holding a supreme rule over most, and when Queen Visa had tried to resist their influence or turn others against them, she'd met much resistance. And their Warriors! They were always creating problems for the queen and her fae. However, that was all about to change. With no police enforcing laws, the world could work the way it was supposed to: in complete chaos.

Because of the House of Seven, Queen Visa had been

unable to overrun the elves in the Pacific. The gnomes had refused to work with her, on the advice of a Warrior, and they had stepped in every time she'd tried to eliminate the fairy population.

And then a treasure had strolled into Queen Visa's kingdom, changing everything.

When Warrior Beaufont had first tried to negotiate with the queen, she'd had no intention of complying. Then the dumb girl had offered Queen Visa the one thing she'd been looking for a long time: her blood.

Yes, she could have killed the magician on the spot. That would have been momentarily satisfying, but it wouldn't serve any long-term good. Queen Visa had tried spilling a Warrior's blood at the threshold of the House of Seven, but it had done nothing, not opening the door for her. She'd had to dispose of the pest in the kingdom of the Fae so the council didn't figure out what she was trying to do. That was when she'd realized that the blood of a Royal had to be freely given in order to work.

And the idiot magician had strolled into her kingdom and given her exactly what she needed to destroy the House of Seven.

Queen Visa stood on the boardwalk outside the faux entrance to the House in Santa Monica, her long red dress billowing in the wind as the Pacific Ocean crashed on the shore at her back. She patted the head of the large black bear sitting next to her on his leash. Bruiser was Queen Visa's most trusted companion. She treasured no one more than the bear, who had been by her side during every battle for the last three hundred years. Bruiser would ensure that the destruction of the House and its Royals was swift. No one would be left alive when they were done.

Lame mortals strode around the queen of the fae, thinking she was walking a large dog. They never saw things for what they were because they lacked intelligence. Queen Visa's first act after destroying the House of Seven would be to eliminate the pesky mortals, something she'd gotten in trouble for many a time based on the House's laws. No more, though.

Maybe she would keep a few mortals alive, but they would be the fae's slaves. The House of Seven was short-sighted in protecting other races. They didn't get that, as the ones with magic, they should be exerting their dominance over the weaker race. The fae were undoubtedly the most powerful of all, but they had been forced to live in the shadows, conforming to ridiculous laws. Queen Visa had had enough. Today that would all change.

She stepped forward, the giant bear following her. When she came to the door of the palm-reading shop, Queen Visa uncorked the vial of Liv Beaufont's blood. With a wicked smile on her face, she emptied the vial on the threshold and waited for the door to swing open, granting her access to the House of Seven.

Nothing happened.

Queen Visa narrowed her eyes, giving it another few seconds.

Still nothing happened, and unstoppable rage coursed through the queen, lighting a white-hot flame inside her.

The door hadn't opened, and that could mean only one thing: this wasn't Liv Beaufont's blood.

Which meant she would soon be dead.

CHAPTER THIRTY-THREE

"You brought us to the *fashion district* in LA?" Liv asked in disbelief, looking at the banner for Santee Alley hanging over a street clogged with mortals shopping for good deals.

Rory gazed around, seemingly trying to locate something on the busy street.

When he didn't answer, Liv said, "Did you need Soph's and my help picking out a suit? Is this where giants get their clothes because they get the best deals on extra-extra-extra-large jeans?"

Rory gave her a patient expression. "We're not here for clothes."

Liv looked down at Sophia, who was wearing a pink-and-white-striped dress jacket buttoned all the way up to her chin. She looked like she'd stepped out of twentieth-century London, with the hat on her head and carrying her parasol. Sophia Beaufont was a timeless beauty who had apparently inherited all the class that had skipped Liv.

"Maybe the giant wants our help picking out some

high-tops," Liv mused in a loud whisper. "I hear one can get good deals if they know how to haggle."

Sophia giggled, her eyes wide as she watched the various characters peddling their wares and trying to get customers to come into their booths.

"I don't wear high-tops," Rory said simply, looking both ways before crossing the street.

"Birkenstocks, then," Liv said at once, crossing with him, holding Sophia's small hand.

He shook his head, towering over the crowd.

"Is this a wardrobe intervention?" Liv asked. "Did your mother put you up to this?"

Rory glared down at her. "It may surprise you, but I don't even notice how you dress. Actually, I hardly notice you, runt."

Liv laughed, glad to finally have gotten a reaction out of him. "How is Mummy? Has she found anything?"

Rory cut his eyes to the side, paranoia written on his face. "I don't think so, but our communication is limited."

"Like you only Facetime morning, afternoon, and evening?" Liv asked, holding tight to Sophia as the crowd around them thickened.

"Speaking of which," Rory began, "I don't think you should go to the Matterhorn yet."

"But the doctor said that a brainwave—"

The scolding look on Rory's face cut her off. "I remember what you told me. No details here. There are many, many magical creatures in this place."

Liv studied the people around them. Most of them appeared to be tourists who liked to buy knockoffs while eating cotton candy. "Where are these magical creatures?"

Rory rolled his eyes. "All over. How do you not see them?"

Taking another glimpse around, Liv immediately spied what he meant, almost like his words had made them appear. Hanging out in a row of handbags were fearsome-looking gremlins, who ducked into the purse every time a mortal got too close. Flying between the rafters of a nearby swimsuit shop were fairies, sprinkling sparkly dust on the customers. And the jewelry shop that was filled with mortals was most assuredly run by gnomes. They were all hiding in plain sight, but the mortals didn't even seem to notice them. No one even paid attention to Rory, who towered above the crowd.

"Oh, there they are..." Sophia said, apparently having seen all the magical creatures about the same time that Liv did.

"You're much more observant than your sister," Rory said to the young magician. "Which is why I've agreed to get you this item today. I think you're worthy of it."

"Wait, that was a compliment," Liv argued.

"And?" Rory asked.

"You've never given *me* a compliment," she complained.

"Haven't I?" he asked.

"Oh, that's fine," she said, crossing her arms. "I risk my life to save the giants and get you that sword, and you act like my existence is a constant annoyance to you."

"Act?" he questioned, striding through the alley, many parting to make way for the giant.

"Ha-ha," Liv said. "Well-played, giant. I thought you were allergic to jokes."

"Just bad ones," he retorted. "So, the ones you tell."

"My jokes are fantastic," Liv countered.

"About the Matterhorn," Rory said, his face growing more serious. "We know it's a dangerous place based on what happened to your parents. I think more research needs to be done before you venture there."

Liv nodded. She was antsy to go to this place that could hold answers, but Rory was right that she needed to be careful. "I thought about starting by going to the burned-down beach house where Ian and Reese..." Her voice trailed away when she saw the traumatized expression jump to Sophia's face.

Thankfully she didn't have to finish her sentence. Rory knew what she was referring to. "I think that needs to wait, too. What I think you should do is more research. You don't even know what you're looking for right now, so you might miss it."

"I've been researching," Liv stated, frustration growing in her. With each day that passed, she felt like she was letting her family down by not making progress.

"Yes, but there's still more to do," Rory encouraged, his tone actually sensitive. "You mentioned that bit about John. I think that's worth looking into more."

Liv nodded. "Yes, I'm having him dig up his old family records. And I guess you're right."

"Of course I am," he stated plainly. "If you're caught in either one of those locations, it will throw too much suspicion on you. For now, I actually think you need to take the break the council has given you and relax a little. You've been going nonstop between cases."

He was right, and Liv appreciated the sentiment, even if it wasn't a compliment. She and Trudy had proudly informed the council that they'd remedied the werewolf issue in Lupei and there wouldn't be any more problems. Adler appeared mildly irritated but hid it well, dismissing them both at once, saying they didn't have another case for them yet. Apparently, he'd expected them to be gone for a lot longer. Or killed.

"You did promise to take me for nachos," Sophia said excitedly. "Can we do that?"

Liv beamed. "Good idea! And yes, we'll do that, and I'll teach you how to play video games and board games, and we can—"

Rory held up a hand. "Before you go making a lot of plans, Sophia might be busy after we leave here."

Liv arched an eyebrow at him. "Busy how?"

"I just think she'll have extra responsibility." He glanced down at the little magician. "That's okay with you, isn't it?"

"Oh, yes!" she exclaimed.

"What do you have up your sleeve, Ro?" Liv asked skeptically.

"An arm," he answered matter-of-factly.

Liv was about to make another joke when a short, round woman ran up to Rory, throwing her arms around his waist. It looked like she tried to pick him up as she rocked back on her heels, but he merely tilted slightly, his face blossoming into a fantastic shade of red.

"There's the man who saved my business," the woman said in broken English.

Rory fought to get out of her grasp, but she had her head pressed to his waist and her eyes closed as she squeezed him.

"Oh, this should be interesting," Liv said to Sophia out of the corner of her mouth.

Finally Rory was able to peel the woman off him. "It was nothing," he said to the girls before looking down at the woman. "Ms. Krucken, you're looking well."

The woman wiped tears from her eyes, smiling broadly and revealing several blackened teeth. "Thank you, but if I am, it is only because of your generosity, you big strong man."

"Whatever did you do for this lovely lady?" Liv asked, sidling up next to the woman. Ms. Krucken had several warts on her chin, as well as a fair bit of facial hair.

Rory waved her off, shaking his head at the short woman. "It was nothing, and definitely not something we need to talk about."

"Nothing!" the woman yelled, gaining attention from several passersby. "When this strapping young lad found out my business was going to close, he paid my mortgage for the next two years, giving me the money I needed to keep things going." She wagged a finger at Rory. "The bank wouldn't tell me who did it, but I know it was you. Simon said he saw you in the bank the day before, talking to my account manager, all shush-shush."

"Wow! Is this true, you big, strong man?" Liv asked Rory, who looked like he wanted to crawl into a large hole.

"I don't know what you mean," Rory said, looking around like he was suddenly late for an appointment.

The woman laughed, slapping Rory on the arm. "He knows what he did, and he's a saint. I owe everything I have to him. I plan to repay you as soon as things are better."

Rory shook his head. "No, that's not necessary. Please don't—"

"So you *did* do it," Liv said proudly, grateful to finally have caught him in the act of doing something nice, or kind of.

"No, it's all a misunderstanding," Rory stated in a rush.

"So humble," the woman said, smiling at Liv. "And is this your wife and daughter? They sure are...compact compared to you."

Sophia laughed. Liv grimaced. Rory's red shade deepened.

"I look old enough to be her mother?" Liv asked, pointing at her sister. "I do need to take a break from working so much."

"And take vitamins, and stop eating so many carbs," Rory muttered.

"We're his friends," Sophia said cheerfully. "He's taking me to get a present."

Ms. Krucken clapped her hands together. "Oh, that sounds like my knight in shining armor. Such a blessed soul."

"Well, we better be off," Rory said hurriedly. "Good to see you again, Ms. Krucken. Please take care."

He grabbed Liv, who had a hold of Sophia's hand, by the back of her collar and dragged them through the horde of people. When they had reached a less congested area, he released them, looking like he'd just run a marathon.

Liv gave him a huge smile and winked. "You really are a man of mystery, aren't you, you big, strong knight?"

CHAPTER THIRTY-FOUR

Apparently, Rory didn't like any of the jokes Liv told as they wove their way through the open market. His expression remained sour as he kept his head down, like he might be recognized by someone again and have more of his secrets exposed. Liv kept a tight hand on Sophia, not releasing her even when they halted in front of a shop that sold hair extensions.

"This is where you're buying my sister a present?" Liv asked, and peered down at her sister. "I'm sort of glad that the giant hasn't taken a shine to me."

"I'm not buying Sophia hair extensions," Rory said dryly, looking around the store as if trying to locate someone.

"Oh, they are for you, then?" Liv quipped. "I'm not sure they will be able to match those curly brown locks of yours, but maybe if you get a Brazilian blowout and have it straightened, they can pair it up with something that blends in."

Rory shot her a mock-contemptuous glare. "You are seriously ridiculous. You do realize that, right?"

Liv spun around, searching for the person he was referring to. When she didn't find anyone, she turned back, pointing to herself. "You mean me? I'm the ridiculous one? I'm the only one in this group not attracting attention to myself because I'm unbelievably adorable or abnormally huge, and *I'm* the strange one between the three of us? Yeah, okay."

"Come on," Rory said, striding into the shop toward the back, where a small Asian woman was standing behind a counter.

"Ooki," the woman exclaimed when she caught sight of Rory. "It's been so long. How have you been?"

Rory bowed to her humbly with a fake smile on his face. "I'm well. And you?"

The woman's eyes slid to Liv and Sophia as she nodded. Although her ears were glamoured, Liv knew she was an elf. For some reason, Liv got the distinct impression of water when she looked at the woman, which was the element that elves controlled and pulled from. This must have been how others had recognized her as a magician before she introduced herself. They must have just been able to feel her unique brand of magic.

"Is Shin here?" Rory asked.

"Yes, he's in the back," the woman said, nodding to a curtain behind her.

Rory sidled around her and headed in that direction. Liv went to follow with Sophia in tow, but the woman stepped into their path and stopped them with a single hand.

"Ooki, can you vouch for these two?" the woman asked him, her eyebrows arching.

"Yes. The smaller one is fine, and the other one is a pain in the butt but still completely fine," he answered.

"They won't talk?" the woman questioned.

"Talk about what?" Liv asked.

The woman ran skeptical eyes over her. "We don't like others to know what we sell back there. It's private, and by invite only. Ooki has been invited, and if he vouches for you, you can go back there, but only if you don't tell anyone that we're here. We don't need the wrong types of people noticing us."

Liv nodded, wondering what the hell they were getting themselves into. "Yeah, we'll keep it hush-hush. Don't worry."

Seemingly satisfied by this, the woman stepped aside, allowing Liv and Sophia to pass.

They followed Rory through a back curtain, where he had to duck down a narrow, dark hallway made of fabric curtains.

"What was that all about?" Liv asked.

"This shop, Zuma Zat, sells rare and hard-to-find things," Rory explained in a whisper. "They don't want the wrong types in here or to get attention for the stuff they sell."

"Is it illegal?" Liv asked.

"Maybe by House of Seven standards," Rory explained. "However, not for the rest of the magical community. And while we're talking about it, don't mention that you're a Warrior. That's the last thing we need."

"You know, one day I'm going to find out what you do

for a living and then tell you that you can't talk about it because it's taboo."

Rory shook his head. "Seriously, how do you not know what I do? After all the time we've spent together?"

Liv looked over her shoulder at Sophia. "Am I missing something?"

She shrugged in response.

"All I ever see you do is keep secrets and pretend you don't do nice things for others," Liv stated. "Are you a goodwill ninja of sorts?"

"Seriously ridiculous," Rory said, straightening up as they came to the end of the hallway.

The dim blue light of the shop was actually bright for a moment compared to the corridor they'd come through. Rory was almost able to straighten all the way when they arrived in a large tent with a pitched roof, his head barely grazing the ceiling.

Liv was overwhelmed by the array of strange and interesting objects displayed all over the place. Weird flowers that were full of corkscrews and spikes sat in vases on the far wall. Music that made Liv both sleepy and alert came from a flute hovering in the air like it was being played by an invisible elf. Gems and crystals hung from the ceiling, making it look like a starry sky overhead, and sparkling objects seemed to call for attention from all over the shop.

Liv had seen many strange things on Roya Lane, but nothing like this. It would take days to browse through the strange assortment of magical items in Zuma Zat, but Rory didn't appear the least bit interested in any of it as he marched farther into the shop.

"Ooki!" a short elfish man greeted him, clapping his

hands together. He wore flowing pajama pants, and a round hat on his bald head. His face was partially obscured by a black goatee and a skinny handlebar mustache. "It is good to see you. What brings you here? Need more artifacts? Another transport stone? Or do you want a candle that cleans out a space?" He indicated to a row of candles that were hovering in the air beside the far wall.

Liv strode in that direction and took a whiff, but immediately regretted it. The candles smelled like a mixture of dirty feet and tuna fish. "I'm not sure about cleaning out a space as much as clearing a room of people."

Shin regarded her with mild curiosity, as if he were trying to figure her out. Rory leaned down and whispered in the man's ear, and his eyes sparked with interest.

"For you, Ooki?" Shin asked him. "You know they don't take to your type. Pardon me for saying this, but you're much too big."

Rory shook his head. "No, it's for a magician. If it will work at all, that is."

"Yes," Shin said speculatively. "We'd have to see about that. But yes, just follow me to the back."

Liv went to trail after them, but Rory stopped her. "You two stay here. We'll be right back. And don't touch anything."

The two men disappeared into the back, and Liv gave Sophia a goofy expression. "Don't touch anything," she said, mocking the giant. "Is it strange that they just went to the back of a shop, which is in the back of another shop?"

The girl laughed, walking over to the strange flowers on the wall. "I wonder what these do?"

Liv was about to say that she didn't know when she

recognized the strange markings on the petals. She'd read about them in *Mysterious Creatures*. "Oh, stay back from those," she warned. "Those are chusetor. It's a rare flower that causes hallucinations and other mental disorders. It's used in potions."

Sophia took a large step back. "That's good to know." As she continued to browse a case of artifacts, she said, "Do you know much about potions work?"

Liv shook her head. "It's on the list of things to learn about. Maybe you can help me since you have some experience with it."

"Yes, I'd be happy to," Sophia replied. "And they are really great for hiding magic use, just like many of the objects here."

Liv took a closer look. The case was filled with gems, jewelry, and many things she'd never seen before. There was a busy bee clip like the one Bermuda had given her, and a bunch of stones that looked familiar. Liv pulled the one Rudolf had given her for summoning him from her pocket, and they were the same. Beside those were bowls of flower-petal-looking objects that she recognized as depours. Stefan had given Sophia a blue one that apparently created snow.

"What do the red ones do again?" Liv asked, pointing at the depours.

"They create fire," Sophia answered. "And the purple ones make it rain."

"And they are untraceable?" Liv questioned.

"I think so," Sophia stated. "Although when I used the one Stefan gave me, there were bits of the depour left behind after the snow melted."

"So there's evidence left behind," Liv mused, not sure why this would be of interest to her, although it was.

"I wonder what she does?" Sophia said, leaning down to inspect a small figurine of a woman who was knitting. She was about the size of Liv's hand and made of copper.

The woman's face snapped up to gaze at Sophia. "Would you mind? I'm trying to work. Unless you purchase me, I must return to my work for my master."

Sophia hopped back in alarm.

"That's a bulster," Shin said, striding back into the main area of the shop, Rory following him, carrying a small trunk. "It's made out of clay and cast in metal and then enchanted. She isn't real, but the work she does is. She's my servant, and is currently making me a sweater since my other ones don't fit."

"Ummm," Liv mused. "Unless you're on a diet, I'm not sure this one will fit either."

Shin shook his head at her, stopping beside the figure and holding out his hand. "Bulster, show me your work."

The garment in the statue's hands vanished, and in Shin's fingers appeared a gray, wool sweater. He held it up, inspecting it. "Yes, this is looking good. Hopefully, it won't stretch out like the others. Keep going, and then clean the shop."

The statue nodded as the sweater disappeared from Shin's grasp and reappeared in the woman's copper hands.

"Wow, that's incredibly helpful," Liv stated. "How much?"

"She's not for sale," Shin said. "She's my personal assistant, and I can't stand to lose her. Bulsters are incredibly rare."

"Well, let Ooki know if you ever get another one, because I need someone to personally assist me," Liv stated.

The small Asian man gave Rory a skeptical glare. "This is the one you want to test?" he asked, pointing at Liv.

Rory shook his head, indicating Sophia. "No, it's her."

"Oh, good," Shin said with relief. "You know they don't like humor. Well, at least most don't. Each is different. It depends on many factors."

"What are we talking about?" Liv interjected.

Rory set the trunk in front of Sophia and knelt beside her. Even on his knees, he was taller than her. "I'm going to open this trunk, and what I want you to do is hover your hand over each of the objects inside. Don't touch them, though. Simply put your hand close, and let us know if you feel any of them pulling at you. Does that make sense?"

Sophia looked back at Liv as if asking permission.

"What's in the trunk?" Liv questioned.

"You'll find out," Rory stated. "But first I need Sophia to clear her mind. Can you do that for me?"

The little magician nodded adamantly. "Yes, I can."

"Okay, good," Rory said. "Are you ready?"

"I think so," Sophia answered.

"Take a deep breath and try to relax," Rory urged as he unlocked the trunk and peeled back the lid.

Liv didn't know what she expected to see in the trunk, but what she saw definitely wasn't it. Sitting on thick blue velvet fabric were six large, shimmering eggs, all about the size of cantaloupes.

"Wait," she interjected before Sophia stuck out her

hand, making the girl pause. "Are those what I think they are? I thought they were extinct, or mostly, or something."

Rory shook his head, his attention focused on Sophia. "We'll get to that later. For now, Sophia, focus."

She complied, hovering her hand over the first one, which was a deep red and covered in flakes of gold. After several long seconds, Sophia looked at Rory uncertainly.

"Anything?" he asked hopefully.

She shook her head.

"Then move on," he encouraged, his gaze flicking up to Shin with slight disappointment.

Sophia's hand glided over the next egg, which was a dark emerald green.

"I don't feel any—" Sophia's words were cut off when her hand seemed to be yanked across the trunk to the far corner, where it hovered over the largest of all the eggs, an iridescent blue one. "What just happened?" she asked, looking up at Rory with astonishment.

He gave Shin a satisfied expression. "She's been magnetized. I knew it."

Shin nodded appreciatively. "That you did. But don't get excited yet."

"Excited about what?" Sophia asked, her hand still hovering above the egg.

Rory gave her a compassionate look. "There's a chance that it still might not hatch for you even if magnetized. There are a lot of unknown factors."

Sophia's face was covered in uncertainty.

"You're not seriously thinking of giving my little sister one of these?" Liv asked, glaring at Rory.

"Ooki has already purchased it." Shin said it like it was a done deal.

"Liv, it magnetized to her just like I knew it would," Rory argued. "But really all I'm giving her is an opportunity."

"This isn't like a puppy, where the worst he'll do is tear up the pillows on the couch," Liv fired back.

"Guys," Sophia said, looking between them. "What are you talking about?"

A few days ago, Liv wouldn't have recognized the eggs, but she'd been doing her homework. "My friend here wants to give you a very dangerous pet."

"It's only an egg. Don't worry so much," Rory said dismissively.

"What am I supposed to do with an egg?" Sophia asked.

"Crack it on the side of a frying pan and scramble it," Liv said with a laugh, earning a contemptuous glare from Rory.

"Okay, sorry, bad joke, but seriously, this is your present to her?"

"She's right for it," Rory countered. "I just know it. I had a feeling about this."

"Could you have told me about this feeling first?" Liv asked.

"I didn't know if it would magnetize to her." Rory pointed. "But look, it obviously has, and Shin will tell you that we can't ignore this."

"Ooki is right," Shin stated. "I haven't seen this happen in quite some time. I've had these eggs for longer than I can remember."

"I still don't like this," Liv stated, her hands on her hips.

"She's going to keep this in the House? What if someone finds out about it?" Liv glanced at Shin, worried she'd given something away, but he seemed to think she was simply referring to a house in general.

"Sophia is a master of disguise," Rory stated. "If anyone can hide something like this, it will be her."

"What about when it's the size of a large truck?" Liv asked. "What is she going to do with it then?"

"Well, it will move to the mountains or the ocean," Rory answered. "They aren't meant to live in captivity. Then it will only visit."

"That one will most likely live by the ocean," Shin offered. "Probably on a deserted beach nearby."

"Guys," Sophia said again. "Will someone please tell me what's going on?"

Liv pointed. "Those are dragon eggs."

Sophia's face brightened. "I knew it! And one of them has magnetized to me?"

Rory affirmed. "Yes, which I suspected would happen."

"She's a child," Liv fired. "You're going to give her a dragon?"

"It's right for her," Rory stated. "She has the right temperament. She's incredibly intelligent and patient. I knew that if I gave her the chance, this would happen. And like Shin said, this is rare. Also, not only is it important for someone to bond with the dragon before it hatches, it's even better if the person is young. That allows them to grow up together."

"Yes. If this works," Shin began, "it could make for a perfect pairing."

"And Liv, you don't understand how rare it is that Sophia has been magnetized," Rory continued.

"It's true," Shin stated. "I've had these eggs for over a hundred years. I gave up hope that someone would magnetize to one. But still, we must not get ahead of ourselves, which is why I keep my excitement at bay. The egg must still hatch, and that will only happen under the right circumstances, if at all."

"Right circumstances?" Sophia questioned, doubt covering her face.

"You'll have to care for the egg," Rory stated. "And a lot of that is guesswork. But if the dragon desires, it will hatch for you, and you'll raise it."

"Me?" Sophia asked, sounding both nervous and excited.

"Seriously, Ro, what were you thinking?" Liv began. "Dragon riders have dangerous lives, and live away from others. They are an elite group. That's the life you're offering my sister?"

He smirked slightly. "I'm glad to see you're finally reading *Mysterious Creatures*. And yes, dragon riders do have different lives, but there also hasn't been a new one in over a hundred years. If Sophia's dragon hatches, there's a real possibility that she'll go on to do incredible things. This is a true honor."

"Ooki is right," Shin stated. "I was saddened for a long time, thinking the artform had died. This gives me true hope, although I'm reserving my joy until the dragon actually hatches. That could take another century, or not happen at all. These things are impossible to tell."

"But you just said that they needed to grow up together?" Liv questioned.

Rory nodded. "That would be ideal, but we can't make it happen."

Sophia's hand hovered over the blue egg. "What should I do?" she asked, giving Liv an earnest expression.

She thought for a moment and shook her head. Liv didn't want her little sister to be disappointed if the egg didn't hatch, and then there were the whole set of implications if it did. And then there was the House, and hiding the dragon, which would grow up to be a monster by some standards. But at the end of it, this was Sophia, and she was the brightest light in all the world and deserved to have a choice here.

"This isn't my decision to make, Soph. It's up to you. If this is what you truly want, I'll support it. But do this because you want to and not because you feel pressured to," Liv warned. "Dragons live an incredibly long time, so this isn't something you should enter into lightly. If that dragon hatches, you'll be connected to it all your life."

"Liv is correct," Rory stated. "You have to want this. Doing this with half your heart will lead to dangerous consequences. Dragon magic is volatile, and completely disrupted by uncertainty."

Sophia's gaze drifted to the floor as she thought. She didn't say another word, but simply let her hand fall onto the egg, sealing the bond she'd established with it. The egg glowed under her fingers, making a soft humming sound that dissipated as the egg dimmed again.

Rory smiled so widely that he showed a row of teeth,

his canines pronounced. Liv had never seen him so happy. "This is wonderful. The magnetizing is complete."

"That it is," Shin said, striding forward carrying a thick fabric bag. "Here, you can take it home in this."

Sophia tried to work her fingers around the egg to pick it up. "It's really heavy. Liv, will you help me lift it?"

Shin shook his head. "Oh, no. From this moment forward, you are the only one who can touch the egg. If someone else does, it won't hatch for you. Or if it does, it won't be bonded to you."

"What does that mean?" Sophia asked.

"It means it will try and bite your hands off," Liv joked.

"It means that you have to care for the egg yourself, keeping it close to you and watching over it," Rory offered.

Sophia was able to push the bag around the egg and pull it up, although it hovered only inches from the floor. "Okay, I can do that. I promise to take good care of it. And don't worry, Liv, everything is going to work out. I'll be careful."

Liv stared down at her little sister, nervous but also excited for her. The egg had been magnetized to her, and Rory was right. There was something incredibly special about Sophia Beaufont. If there was to be a new dragon rider in a hundred years, there was no doubt that it would be the incredible magician before her.

CHAPTER THIRTY-FIVE

When Liv entered John's electronic shop, he and Sophia were sitting on either side of the workbench, staring in awe at the blue dragon's egg laying in the center of the table.

"They are exactly where I left them," she said to Plato as she set down the to-go order she'd just picked up from the Mexican restaurant down the block.

The feline didn't answer because it was a game he was playing with Liv to make her look crazy in front of John. She didn't much care for the game.

"I still can't believe it," John said in awe. "There's a real dragon in there."

"I know," Sophia agreed in a similar voice. "It doesn't feel real."

"What does your book say about getting it to hatch?" John asked.

Sophia pulled her copy of *Mysterious Creatures* to her, studying the page she had opened. Liv should have seen this dragon business coming because the last couple days, every time she'd open *Mysterious Creatures*, it would be to a chapter on dragons. Damn Bermuda, and the strangeness of her book.

"It's not clear," Sophia began, reading. "It says to keep it warm, but not too warm. And to keep it clean, but not too clean. And that it needs fresh air, but—"

"Not too much fresh air," Liv cut in, unpacking the containers of food. "Oh, is it a wonder that Rory makes hardly any sense, having been raised by the woman who wrote that book?"

"I can't believe it could take another hundred years for that thing to hatch," John remarked.

"If it does at all," Sophia said, leaning in Liv's direction, her nose leading the way.

"Maybe it just needs some nachos," Liv suggested. "I know I'd break out of my shell to get some of this goodness."

She opened the container, offering it to Sophia. The crispy chips were covered in melted cheese and piled high with *carne asada*, *pico de gallo*, guacamole, and lettuce. "Are you ready to try nachos?"

"Yes," Sophia declared, picking up a single chip all proper-like, as if she were lifting a teacup into the air, her finger extended. She took a small bite, her eyes lighting up with delight. "Wow, those are the best things I've ever tasted!"

"I told you," Liv stated triumphantly, pulling a chip free from its brethren, a string of cheese reaching between the two. Unlike Sophia, she crammed it into her mouth, enjoying the burst of flavor.

"Don't worry, John," Liv said, sliding a container in his direction. "I didn't forget about you."

He rubbed his hands together excitedly. "Can't wait to dig into this double-steak chimichanga with extra-hot salsa."

"About that," Liv said between bites. "I altered the order just a little bit."

His enthusiastic expression dropped. "Why'd you do that?"

"Because your order was a heart attack waiting to happen, and I can't have that," Liv explained. "Instead I got you something similar, but with a little less meat, a few more vegetables, and nothing fried."

John opened the container and grimaced. "What is this?"

"Spinach and chicken enchiladas with a side salad," Liv answered.

He eyed their nachos with envy. "Those look better."

"We're hardly able to choke them down," Liv said, fighting Sophia for more steak pieces.

"What's in there?" John asked, pointing to the other container sitting next to Liv.

"More nachos," she answered. "I told Sophia I wouldn't share with her, but that's not the sisterly thing to do, so I got us two orders. When we finish these, we can move on to more."

John took a bite, not at all looking happy about his meal. "I wish I were a magician who could eat ten thousand calories a day and not have to worry about my heart."

"Speaking of which," Liv said, "have you had a chance to look into the family records like I mentioned?"

After visiting Dr. Dowling's office, Liv had started to piece together a hypothesis about why John could see magic but other mortals couldn't. It might explain why the brain waves being transmitted, if that were in fact the case, didn't affect him.

"Not yet," he answered. "But I will straight after lunch if you don't mind watching the shop while I dig around in the storage area."

"Not at all," Liv said. "That will give me a chance to teach Sophia how to—"

Liv didn't have a chance to finish her sentence, because at that moment a portal appeared in the open space next to the row of shelves. It appeared the same as all other portals, full of blues and greens.

She expected Clark to step through with a sour expression, which would deepen once he found out about the dragon. She even expected that Stefan might be visiting, since he'd been threatening to stop by her other place of work. Or it could have been Hester, who had wanted to check on Liv's injuries after Vera had attacked her.

Get the summoning stone, a voice yelled in Liv's head. She glanced down at Plato and knew immediately that it was him. She did as he said, reaching into her pocket and wrapping her fingers around the stone Rudolf had given to her.

Out of all the things Liv might have expected, she had never pictured a large black bear with a thick collar on a leash stepping through the portal. And even more surprising was that holding his leash was the most beautiful woman in the world: Queen Visa of the fae.

CHAPTER THIRTY-SIX

The first time Liv had seen Queen Visa in the kingdom of the Fae, she was so beautiful it had hurt to look at her, but somehow she appeared even more radiant now as she stepped in the repair shop wearing a backless red gown that flowed behind her like she was being blasted by a fan at a photoshoot. Her long blonde hair cascaded down her back, and her eyes smoldered with hot contempt.

"Warrior Liv Beaufont," she said, her tone full of acid. "Prepare to die for what you've done."

If Liv had had any chance of believing that the queen had merely stopped by for a visit, that was gone now. When they'd first met, Queen Visa had been quite taken with her, stating that they should grab a drink or get massages soon, but apparently, they were no longer friends.

Liv stepped forward, trying to put as much distance between her and the others as possible. "Queen Visa, I can explain if you only give me a chance."

The black bear rose on his back legs, towering as he growled. Until recently, Liv would have said he was the largest animal that she'd ever seen, but werewolves actually rivaled his size.

"I agree, Bruiser," the queen said to the bear. "It is sad that I'll have to kill such a beautiful specimen, but that's what happens when someone lies to me. You didn't give me your blood. There will be no explanations for you, Warrior. You'll pay for what you've done, and so will everyone you care about."

Liv held out her arms protectively. "No, please leave them out of this. They didn't do anything wrong. Just punish me."

"No," Sophia argued and bravely came around to stand in front of her sister, protecting her.

Queen Visa wasn't swayed by this act of courage. She probably would have killed them both on the spot, but the dragon's egg on the workbench caught her attention. "What is that?"

Liv's mind raced. She needed to get Sophia and John out of there, but there was so much going on. She didn't know how she'd manage it. While she had a chance, Liv placed a shielding spell on them. It wouldn't hold for long, but it was the best she could do under the circumstances.

"It's a dragon's egg. I'll give it to you if you like," Sophia said. "All you have to do is let us go."

Liv's heart was lightened by her little sister's act of bravery and selflessness.

However, Queen Visa wasn't impressed. "Child, why would I let you go in exchange for the egg when I could simply take it?"

"Because it's mine," Sophia said boldly. "If you take it, the dragon won't hatch for you, but if I give it to you, it might."

Queen Visa considered this, lowering her chin and running scrutinizing eyes over Sophia. "You are as beautiful as your sister. What is your name, little one?"

Liv ran her fingers over the summoning stone, wondering why Plato had told her to hold onto it. Then the words from *Mysterious Creatures* came back to her, and the strange chapter she had read about fae made more sense all of a sudden:

The fae do have some weaknesses that their adversaries can exploit in order to weaken them. However, the best defense against a fae is another fae. Whereas magicians and elves struggle to penetrate their tough exterior, another fae has little problem getting past these shields. It is for this reason that the fae rarely battle one another, knowing that the biggest weakness to their brand of magic is one of their own. The fae have little history of civil war because of this fact, knowing that if they turned on one another, they would be extinct in no time.

The realization hit Liv hard. She actually *needed* Rudolf. Without him, there was no possible way to defeat the queen of the Fae.

"My name is Sophia Beaufont," the little magician answered, curtseying to the queen. Even when facing a deadly enemy, she was still polite.

Queen Visa took note of her manners too, smiling wickedly. "Maybe I'll only kill Liv and the mortal. I like the idea of having you as one of my pets."

"But you could have my dragon," Sophia argued.

"I don't want your dragon," the queen countered. "Not when I can have you."

Liv slid in front of her sister, having had enough time to formulate her plan. "Sophia isn't up for discussion, and neither is killing me."

The queen's eyes grew hot again as she tightened her grip on the bear's leash. "Bruiser, can you believe how she speaks to me?"

Liv tuned the queen out and focused, gripping the stone. *Come on, Rudolf, I need your help.*

The form of Rudolf sprang up in front of Liv, his back to the queen and Bruiser.

"Well, hey there, love," he chirped, looking at the table. "Having a fiesta and want me to join? I do make everything more fun."

Liv shook her head adamantly.

Rudolf must have caught the seriousness in her eyes because he froze, his smile dropping.

"There's something dangerous and deadly behind me, isn't there?" he asked.

She nodded.

He sniffed the air. "And it reeks of B.O. and garbage…" A moment later he added, "Oh, and I smell a bear as well."

Liv deflated. *Maybe calling on the fae to help hadn't been such a good idea.* She remembered now how he had cowered in front of the queen when they were in Las Vegas. Rudolf had obviously lost his confidence when Queen Visa struck down Serena and buried her at the bottom of the fountain at the House of Seven. But if what Bermuda said about fae was correct, Liv didn't stand a chance without him. On a good day, she could outthink the queen, but everything was happening so suddenly. Her only hope was to open a portal beside the House of Seven and get Sophia and John to safety.

Rudolf pressed his hands into the lapels of his maroon jacket and mouthed the phrase, "I got this." Then he spun to face the queen. "Oh, yes, I totally knew it was you, Visa. You haven't gotten that gland issue taken care of yet, have you?"

The queen's porcelain-white face flushed red. "Rudolfus, why do you look like you've aged? What have you done to yourself?"

Rudolf set off on a path around the queen, snaking behind her and talking over her shoulder. "Why, indeed? Do you remember when you murdered the woman who would have been my wife on our wedding day?"

Queen Visa, undeterred by his closeness, batted her eyelashes. "And here I worried that you'd forgotten all the nice things I've done for you."

When Rudolf came around to the other side of the queen, he stuck his face up next to the bear, seeming to have a staring contest with it. "Well, I managed to get Serena's body out of the fountain where you accidentally left it, you silly blonde."

"You *what*?" Queen Visa said in disbelief. "How could you do that..." Her eyes swiveled to Liv. "You! *You* helped Rudolfus to get that tramp back? Now you're really going to pay."

Liv knew Visa was a woman of her word, which meant time was running out. She had to get Sophia and John out of the shop. Hopefully, Rudolf would create a distraction for her to do it since that was what he was good at.

As if sensing her thoughts, he pulled his face away from the bear and glared at the queen. "The bear has much better-smelling breath than you."

Liv almost laughed but instead took this opportunity to open a portal behind Sophia.

"What are you doing, girl?" Queen Visa yelled. "You'll die *now* for this." She raised a hand, seconds away from ending Liv's life.

The Warrior turned to usher Sophia through the portal, but a loud roar cut through the air. Liv spun to find that where Plato had been standing was a large black panther. It leapt through the air and attacked the bear, who growled furiously. The panther had the advantage, wrestling the bear onto its back and swatting it in the face.

"No! Bruiser!" the queen yelled. "Get off of him, you beast."

Liv took this chance to shove Sophia through the portal and ordered John to follow. He didn't move fast, his face white and his eyes filled with horror. Once they were through, she closed the portal and turned to find the panther and the bear rolling around, knocking into the shelves, appliances raining down on them.

"You dirty lynx!" Queen Visa screamed. "I'll kill you for this!"

"No!" Liv yelled and strode forward, but Rudolf cut her off with a devilish grin.

"I've got this, love," he said, pushing her aside. "Visa, you've gone too far, oppressing your people. Holding us back. It's time you were stopped for your treachery." He held up his hand, about to spell the queen, when she shot a single look at him, making him falter and clutch his chest like he was having a heart attack.

"Rudolf," Liv said, diving forward to catch him before he hit the ground.

"I'm okay," he said in a hoarse whisper as she led him to the workbench, which he used for support.

"No, he's not," the queen stated. "He's too weak to face me. You've always been too weak, Rudolfus. We both know that. I took your confidence long ago, and now I'll take your life."

Liv knew they were out of options. Plato was maintaining his own in the fight as he and the bear exchanged assaults, but how long would that last?

"What exactly do you want?" Liv asked. "Do you want my blood? I'll give it to you. Just leave us alone."

Plato suddenly had the upper hand on the bear, delivering a punishing blow. Bruiser cried, rolling over and covering his head with his paw like he was begging for mercy.

"You good-for-nothing lynx," the queen spat. "I'll take care of you next, after your master."

Rudolf sputtered out a cough and pushed himself upright. "No, Liv. You can't give her your blood. She's too dangerous."

The queen smiled ruefully. "It's true, I *am* too dangerous, which is why it's laughable that you ever thought you could face me, Rudolfus. As your punishment for going against me and bringing back that little slut Serena, I'm going to kill your friend and make you watch. Then I'll end you very, very slowly."

She dipped her finger in the air as if playing musical

SARAH NOFFKE & MICHAEL ANDERLE

notes on invisible keys. Liv had no idea how to get out of this, and strangely, most of her being screamed to stay put.

"No, you wicked bitch," Rudolf said, striding forward and sending a spell at the queen. Her hand froze in the air, and her eyes jerked to the side—and then, to Liv's horror, she simply laughed.

"You've partially frozen me, but that won't last for long," she said. "You're so weak, Rudolfus. You can't even do one thing right."

"That might have been true before," he began, his voice fierce. "But not anymore. I have my confidence back. And better than that, I have friends."

Rudolf held out his other hand beside him and glanced over his shoulder at Liv. She didn't know what he wanted at first, and then it occurred to her. He wasn't strong enough to kill Queen Visa, and she wasn't either, but together, they might stand a chance.

Liv took a giant step forward and locked hands with the fae. Rudolf's hand grew hot in hers as he began to recite words she didn't understand. They sounded like power and mystery. Like the things dreams were born from and fairy-tales were made of. Instantly power streamed from his outstretched hand, covering the queen in frost. It embraced her legs, her hips, and her torso, rising steadily.

"No! No! No!" She screamed, and it was so loud that it burst the display windows in the front of the shop, sending glass everywhere. However, Liv didn't even shield herself, only kept her power steadily streaming to Rudolf as he continued to chant. The frost covered the queen's chest and neck, rising faster up her face and then covering her completely. It was so strange to stare at the frozen queen,

266

and Liv didn't know what would happen next, until there was an explosion of ice. Queen Visa shattered into thousands of pieces of ice like a sculpture, scattering all over the floor and melting almost instantly.

Liv was briefly aware that Plato was standing over the bear and that her ears were ringing. She was afraid to pull her hand from Rudolf's, not sure if she could remain standing without his help.

He turned to her with a proud smile. "And now I can mark that off my to-do list."

Liv was about to rejoice when the fae stumbled forward like he was drunk. She went to catch him but realized she was much too weak. Instead, the two of them slid to the floor as one, passing out in a puddle of ice water left by Queen Visa.

CHAPTER THIRTY-SEVEN

"Try fanning her," a voice urged.

"No, just shake her," someone else stated.

"You two be quiet, or I'm going to put a silencing spell on you," a woman threatened.

Liv felt a steady stream of energy flowing into her from the hand clasped in hers. When her reserves were partially restored, she forced her eyes to open, but they only fluttered.

"That's it, my dear," Hester said. The healer was sitting just in front of her. She realized then that the healer was funneling energy into her, similar to how Rudolf had taken it from her reserves. "You're almost there. Just keep trying to come back to us."

Drawing a deep breath, Liv opened her eyes, blinking to try to make the blurry figures take proper form.

"There you are," Hester said, pulling Liv to a seated position.

Behind one of her shoulders was Clark, who didn't look happy at all about things. Behind the other shoulder was

Stefan, who was looking her over like she might have other injuries.

"Sophia!" Liv half-screamed, her heart suddenly racing.

Hester patted her hand thoughtfully. "She's just fine. So is that mortal…"

"His name is John," Clark offered. "They are in the back of the shop."

Liv glanced around and was surprised to find the black bear lying as he'd been before, his paw covering his head. Beside him Plato was in his usual form, casually licking his own paw.

Feeling the warmth of another body next to her, Liv found Rudolf sitting next to her. "Hey, are you okay?"

"He's fine," Hester answered for him. "Fae recover much faster than magicians. I didn't even have to do anything for him. He awoke on his own."

Liv wasn't sure what possessed her, but she threw her arms around Rudolf, hugging him to her. "We did it. I mean, you did."

He pulled her in tighter. "No, it was you. I couldn't have done it without your help."

"About that," Clark interjected, his tone clipped.

Liv separated from the fae and got ready for the lecture. "How could you face the queen of the Fae like that? You could have gotten yourself killed!"

"Well, I didn't really have a choice, now did I?" Liv countered. "I got Sophia and John out of here, but there was nothing else I could do."

"You did well, getting them to safety," Clark commended her. "Sophia came straight to me and told me what had happened. You can imagine our panic when we showed up here to find you two passed out and a bear on the floor."

"What subdued the bear, anyway?" Stefan asked.

Liv glanced over her shoulder, meeting Plato's eyes. There was something in his expression that said, "Don't give away my secret."

"I'm not sure," she lied. "A spell of some sort."

"Well, back to the matter at hand," Clark stated. "What you did was…well, it was so *you*. It was infuriating. And spontaneous. And—"

"Completely commendable," Stefan cut in.

"Thank you. And I only did what I had to in order to defeat Queen Visa," Liv explained. "If we hadn't, she wasn't going to stop, because she wanted more power and control. It was only a matter of time before she became too strong for anyone to defeat."

"But offering your reserves to this fae?" Hester said, indicating Rudolf. "That was very risky. If he had siphoned any more, you might not have made it."

"But if she hadn't, we wouldn't have defeated that wicked bitch," Rudolf shot back.

Hester agreed with a nod and then, seeming to change her mind, she bowed. "You're very right, King of the Fae."

"Wait, what?" Liv asked. She poked her ear, thinking she was still asleep. "What did you call him?"

"Well, king of the fae," Hester said. "I apologize, what is your name?"

"Rudolf," he supplied.

"Yes, well, King Rudolf defeated the previous ruler of the fae, and by their laws, that makes him their new leader," Hester explained.

"That's right," Rudolf said victoriously. "I knew today was going to be a good day when I woke up and Serena was going down—"

"King or no king, if you finish that sentence, I will strangle you," Liv threatened.

He shook his head. "Oh, fine, then. I won't tell you about Serena's trip down to the market if you're going to be that way."

"Well, I'll be. I never expected all this. You're a king, although I'm certain you can't cross the street alone," Liv said, holding her hand up to her head and swaying slightly.

"Here, try eating something," Stefan offered, bringing over the container of now-cold nachos.

"I don't mind if I do," Rudolf said, cutting Liv off as she reached for one.

She shook her head. "That's so bizarre. Now you're in charge of your people? I don't have to call you King Rudolf, do I?"

"I'm sure you'll find a way to put your own flare on the title," he said with a wink, grimacing after taking a bite and putting a half-eaten chip back.

"We're going to have to figure out what to do with that bear," Hester said suddenly, looking around.

"I can help with that," Stefan offered.

"Very good," the Councilor said. "And then there's this place... What do you call it?"

"It's an electronics repair shop," Liv supplied. "I work here on the side."

Hester nodded. "Yes, it's very charming. I like it. But it's a mess, and will need to be repaired."

Glass and broken appliances were everywhere. Liv

didn't want John to have to deal with his shop being wrecked again.

"I can take care of that," Clark said, instantly going to work putting things away using his magic.

Hester and Stefan carefully approached the bear, who looked unwilling to move, especially with Plato in front of him giving him a death stare.

Liv pushed up to her feet, nearly slipping in the water on the floor. That was when it really sunk in. "Queen Visa is gone, Rudolf. Can you believe it?"

He stood along with her, brushing off his jacket. "Yes, it's hard to fathom, but the possibilities are now endless. I never expected a great honor such as being king, but now that I am, I plan to do wonderful things."

"Like make Taco Tuesdays a national holiday?" she joked.

He laughed. "Like encourage the fae to use their potential. We've grown so complacent over the years, not utilizing our talents. Letting them waste away. All we do is overindulge and make trouble for mortals. The fae used to be the greatest artists and writers in the world. Pollock, Picasso, O'Keefe."

"Wow, those were all fae?" Liv asked.

He shook his head. "No, those were mortals who became famous because the fae weren't hogging the spotlight."

Liv laughed. "Well, try to leave a little bit of room for the mortals to get some attention."

He bowed humbly. "Of course. And are you prepared for when Serena finds out that you threw yourself at me?"

Liv shook her head. "Tell her I was delirious, and that it

will never happen again. I was certain we were both going to die. But since near-death experiences are now common-place for me, I don't react like I used to."

Rudolf gave her a sympathetic expression. "How about this time, I don't tell her?"

"Sure, that sounds good."

He put his arm around her shoulders, and she allowed him to hug her. They looked at the repair shop being put back together by Clark as Hester and Stefan tried to deal with the bear.

"Thanks for coming to my rescue," Liv said in a hushed voice.

"Thanks for letting me use your power. I couldn't have defeated that awful woman without you."

"You know, Rudolf, you're not so bad, but if you ever tell anyone I said that, I will strangle you."

He leaned his head on her shoulder and smiled. "And you know what, Liv? You're not so bad either. Actually, you're a very loyal friend."

CHAPTER THIRTY-EIGHT

L iv sat on the workbench, kicking her legs, with Plato beside her.

Stefan and Hester had left an hour ago with the black bear. They thought they could take it to a place where it could be rehabilitated and have a chance at a normal life. The shop looked as if nothing had happened. However, Liv didn't feel that same way.

She'd spent the last several minutes trying to wrap her head around the last two battles. They had been eerily similar. In both instances, a race of magical creatures had warred internally, and although Liv was a Warrior for the House of Seven, she hadn't been the one to make peace.

Instead, her job had been to call on someone inside the race. In the case of the werewolves, she'd had to rely on Fane. And with the fae, it was Rudolf who took down the queen. That gave her hope that maybe that was how things would happen for the House. It had fallen apart from within, as empires often do, which meant it had to rely on its own to put it back together.

It would take mortals *and* magicians to fix things. And more than anything, no matter what the future held, Liv wanted to be a part of that change.

"Thank you for saving my life yet again," Liv said, rubbing Plato on the head. He nuzzled into the affection, relishing it.

"Just doing my job," he said matter-of-factly.

"Well, maybe one day, it will be my job to save you."

"If it is, the world has gone to shit, and you should take a spaceship to another planet," he joked, settling down his head like he was taking a nap.

A second later, Clark stormed through the door to the back. "Are you serious? This is too much."

Sophia trailed behind him. Liv had been so excited to see that the girl was okay that she'd whisked her off her feet, making her blush when she first saw her. The little magician had done a fantastic job, going back to the House and finding the right help. Liv cringed at the idea that Adler and Bianca could have shown up. Then she'd be explaining why there was a dragon's egg sitting on the workbench.

"It's not that big a deal," Sophia argued. "It might not even hatch."

"It's going to hatch, Soph," Liv encouraged.

"How could you let her get a dragon's egg?" Clark admonished.

"How could I not?" Liv countered. "And it magnetized to her."

"But what if it *does* hatch? How are we going to hide it? And who is going to train her? And what if—"

"Clark," Liv cut in.

"What?" he asked.

"Breathe," she suggested. "Everything is going to be okay. Sophia is brilliant. And she has us, and we're pretty okay. Just try to relax."

He nodded reluctantly.

Remembering something, Liv summoned her father's cane, offering it to him. "Here, I promised I'd return this."

He shook his head. "No, you keep it for a little while. You might need it. Well, at the rate you're going, you'll definitely need it. Who knows what trouble you'll get into next?"

"I was thinking of picking a fight with hairy centaurs next," she teased.

"Figures," he replied, giving Sophia a look as she gathered up her egg. "Are you ready to go?"

She nodded, blowing a kiss to Liv. "Thanks for the nachos. And the memories. And the laughs."

Liv blew her a kiss back. "Anytime."

"Will I see you tomorrow?" Clark asked as they strode for the door.

"As always." Liv waved to him.

"Try not to get into trouble between now and then," he cautioned.

"Fat chance," she replied.

Liv and Plato enjoyed a full moment of quiet before John pushed through the door at the back, carrying a box, Pickles at his heels.

"Oh, good, I'm glad to see you're looking better," he said, striding over and sliding the box onto the table beside them.

He eyed Plato a bit reluctantly. "Were my eyes deceiving me, or did that cat…"

"Turn into a panther?" Liv supplied. "I told you he can talk."

John shook his head. "I saw him shapeshift. There was no talking going on."

"Yeah, well, maybe one day he'll prove I'm not crazy," Liv stated.

Plato gave her an expression that said, "Don't hold your breath."

"Is it normal for your cat to be able to do that?" John asked.

"What, doesn't Pickles morph into a wolf?"

John laughed. "Only when he's really hungry."

Liv pointed to the box. "What do you have there?"

"Remember, you asked for my family records," John answered.

It was a longshot, Liv realized, but ever since talking to Dr. Dowling, she thought there could be a connection between the ancestors of the Mortal Seven and the ability to see magic. There was still much to uncover on this subject, but she thought that if they could link John to one of the original mortal families even distantly, it might give them a lead.

"My mother had our genealogy done years ago," John explained, pulling a dusty old book from the box. "She was able to trace our family roots all the way back. Pretty fascinating stuff."

Liv pulled up the picture she'd taken of the names of the Mortal Seven in the Ancient Chamber on her phone.

"Okay, look through there and tell me if any of these names are one of your distant relatives."

John scanned the family tree. "Go for it."

"Any Fioris in there?" she asked.

He shook his head.

"How about Wong?"

John laughed. "No. Nothing with Asian descent."

"Okay, what about Gaurmond, Alvarez, or Luce?"

John took a moment before saying, "No."

"All right, well, only two more. Reynolds, or Carloway."

John's eyes widened. "What did you say?"

"Reynolds."

"No, the other name," he said.

"Carloway?" Liv asked. "Is there someone in your family with that name?"

"I'd say," John said, suddenly appearing breathless. "My family can trace their heritage all the way back to the Carloways."

"How is that?" Liv asked.

"We're the Carraways now. At some point long ago, they changed the name, but no one knew why," John explained.

"Maybe to protect them from dangerous magicians," Liv stated. "Or maybe they were forced to in order to cover things up."

John's eyes slid away. "What does this all mean?"

Liv thought for a moment. "Do you have any other living relatives?" She already knew the answer to the question, but she had to ask. John was an only child, and the last of the Carraways.

He shook his head. "No, it's just me."

Everything suddenly came together like a puzzle. It was beautiful and bizarre, and way too strange. With a knot forming in her chest, Liv looked at him meaningfully. "If I'm right about this, John, it could mean you're one of the Mortal Seven."

He slapped his hand to his forehead. "Well, I'll be. I never expected anything like this."

Liv hadn't either. And maybe there were other Carraways in the world, but ones who were descended from the Carloways? No, it made sense that John was one of the Seven, and it absolutely explained why he could see magic as a mortal.

Liv didn't know what the odds were that she'd made friends with one of the Mortal Seven the day she'd left the House. However, as she glanced down at the feline beside her, she realized there was a lot of serendipity in her existence. Plato had come into her life that same day as well. Things had a way of doing that for Liv Beaufont—coming together even when she didn't think the pieces fit.

Remarkably, she was closer to the truth than ever before, but more importantly, she felt hopeful that they could uncover it. She needed to investigate more. That would definitely involve going to Matterhorn. Who knew what she'd find there? Maybe clues? Maybe something her parents left behind?

If the werewolves and fae could fix things amongst themselves, it gave Liv hope that the mortals and magicians could too. She firmly believed that they needed one another the way that she needed John. He created balance in her life. The words inscribed on her ring echoed in her head: Together we are strong and balanced.

Yes, magicians and mortals weren't separate. They were each part of the whole. They might have been divided for a long, long time, but it only took the spirit of one person to mend the rift.

Liv didn't know if she would be the person to stand up for her people, as Fane and Rudolf had done to save their own. However, if called upon, Liv would rise to the challenge.

SARAH'S AUTHOR NOTES
APRIL 15, 2019

I sort of have trauma after writing this book. I was three days ahead of schedule when I was nearing the end. That never, ever happens. Currently, I'm finishing book six and I'm behind and looking at writing thirty thousand words over three days to finish three days late. But with book five, I was ahead of the game. I had it all mapped out. I would write ten thousand words in one day to finish—no easy feat. However, I figured if I did this then I could take those glorious two days to hang out by the pool or Netflix.

So as planned, I finished this book on a Friday. Saved. Sent to Jurgen. And went to veg on the couch. Imagine my horror when at three o'clock in the morning Jurgen messages me to tell me that the new chapters weren't in the book.

What!? Of course they are! You must be mistaken.

I jumped out of bed to get to the bottom of this, knowing I couldn't sleep anymore with the worry circulating in my being. I had words disappear one other time. It was horrible and I thought I'd learned my less, having backup of the backup.

Jurgen was right! The words were gone. I didn't know where they went. The first time this happened, I spent hours trying to figure out what happened. It didn't bring the words back. So at three o'clock in the morning, I began rewriting the words. I'd just written them, so it shouldn't be hard, right? Well, it sucked. All of a sudden I went from having the day off, to having a Ground Hog's Day where I did the exact same thing I did the day before.

But you know what, I think the words are better for it. The ending has to be tighter. I wrote it twice.

On top of this traumatic event, Michael and I had two of the four books in this series disappear from Amazon. Poof! Gone. It happened to many other authors over this crazy weekend, not just us. But man did it suck.

You know who didn't suck? You awesome readers. I had so many people reach out to support us. At first, some readers were annoyed because book four was supposed to be on sale. Not only wasn't it on sale, it was missing. Once I explained that though, readers lavished us with support.

And the next day, I had completed the book (a second time) and the other books were back online. I was exhausted and nervous. However, I felt better for the experience. I proved I could weather the storm and the books got back their best seller tags, proving they could come back from a huge slump. Really I have you all to thank for that. So thank you! I'm glad you're enjoying the series. That keeps me going on days like today when I need to write ten thousand words instead of going outside. It will all be worth the effort when the book is done. Then I'm getting nachos!

Dammit, I want Nachos now.

(By the way, *THANK YOU for reading this book!*)

I'm not going to say ANYTHING about being fortunate and not losing any work recently, in the far past, or 'nothin'. Why? Because there are little demons at work just waiting to hear that stuff and POUNCE on an unsuspecting author and make his life horrible.

Or, you know, mine.

Across the company, we had about six books disappear during those crappy days. Although Amazon got their proverbial 'stuff' together pretty quickly, it was a stressful moment. But never fear, Sarah was here!

She was professional and calm during the whole incident. If she wasn't, I don't remember that aspect, and I would appreciate anyone who would know differently not reminding me.

In my mind, she was perfect.

We both hope you have enjoyed the series. We have

three (3) more books in this arc, then whether we move ahead or not is simply in the fans' hands.

Either way, I thank you all from the bottom of my heart for supporting Sarah as she worked her fingers to the bone with these stories. I believe it was the refreshment her soul needed to see how loved a character, modeled after her snarky petite self, would become to so many people.

This is the first time ANY of my series (as a collaborator or by myself) has had four of the books have simultaneous orange best-seller tags.

That was a very cool sight!

FAN'S NOTES - Where a fan helps me out with THEIR love of reading and we learn a bit more about our fellow readers out here!

Today's fan is: Lesskarr Wolfe from IL USA
About how many books do you read a year, or total in your lifetime?
Too many to count

Name your favorite LMBPN Series or Character(s) and what you like about them.
Katie and Pandora from the *Protected by the Damned* series (Mike: WOOT! I'm excited that they are your favorites. I've come to feel that very little has outshone Bethany Anne, and it's cool to see one of the other characters be someone's favorite.)

If you made up an LMBPN Character, what would be three attributes you would use? (For Example, Bethany Anne is Justice, Family (including friends), and Coca-

Cola. Brownstone is Keeping it Simple, Respect, and BBQ)

Honor, integrity, and loyalty

Tell us a few short sentences about yourself, and your reading hobby (When did you start reading, why, how much do you read and preferred genre's etc. (as ideas)):

I been reading since I was a kid and it's an escape from the drama of RL. (I've read a LOT to try and escape either worries and concerns or just 'veg' after hard times in life and wanting to put life on hold for a few hours.)

You can have my <what?> before you can have my reading time.

Nothing. (Mike: Ok, I can't even think to go here because I keep thinking "what about food? Drink... Restrooms..." (Don't judge me, I love my reading time... but...ewww.))

Place you have loved to read the most in your life - best memories (mine was as a teenager at my grandparents house under the feather bed on cold days.)

In my room on my kindle. (*Mike: One of the greatest devices ever developed with me in mind. I agree.*)

AROUND THE WORLD IN 80 DAYS

One of the interesting (at least to me) aspects of my life is the ability to work from anywhere and at any time. In the future, I hope to re-read my own *Author Notes* and remember my life as a diary entry.

WHERE AM I?

Easy Peasy—Cave in the Sky (™), Las Vegas, Nevada.

Been a busy day, and I'm writing these notes at 9:18PM. I just got through (about an hour and a half ago) talking to two wonderful podcasters, Laurene and Kalene, on *The Writer's Journey*.

I'm finishing these notes and seriously thinking of going to sleep.

FAN PRICING

$0.99 Saturdays (new LMBPN stuff) and $0.99 Wednesday (both LMBPN books and friends of LMBPN books.) Get great stuff from us and others at tantalizing prices.

Go ahead. I bet you can't read just one.

Sign up here: http://lmbpn.com/email/.

HOW TO MARKET FOR BOOKS YOU LOVE

Review them so others have your thoughts, and tell friends and the dogs of your enemies (because who wants to talk to enemies?)... *Enough said ;-)*

Ad Aeternitatem,

Michael Anderle

ACKNOWLEDGMENTS
SARAH NOFFKE

My favorite part of writing any book is creating the acknowledgements page. It reminds me that writing a book is not a solo task. I might sit alone and write, but the finished product is a result of the support and encouragement of a tribe of people.

Thank you to the readers who buy the books, read them, review and recommend. YOU are the one who keeps us writing. I'm always inspired by the messages I receive from readers. Thank you supporting the books and offering so much richness to my life.

Thank you to my LBMPN family for all the support. Steve, Michael, Lynne, Moonchild, Jennifer and so many others who help champion the book to publication and beyond.

Thank you to the beta readers who offered so many valuable insights early on. Thank you to John, Chrisa, Kelly, Martin and Larry.

Thank you to the JIT team for all the awesome feedback. A new series is always exciting and nerve-wracking.

Michael and I thought we had a great idea for a new world, but we don't really know until we get objective feedback. What would I do without all you awesome readers?

Thank you to my friends and family. Writing is a strange profession. I work weird hours, talk to myself, have a strange diet, get antsy about deadlines. But the wonderful people in my life continue to show their encouragement and thoughtfulness no matter what. It is never lost on me because I know that I wouldn't be doing what I love without all you amazing people, cheering me on.

And as with all my books, the final thank you goes to my muse, Lydia. I wrote my first book so that I could make my daughter proud, and it's never stopped. I write every book for you, my love.

Sarah Noffke writes YA and NA science fiction, fantasy, paranormal and urban fantasy. In addition to being an author, she is a mother, podcaster and professor. Noffke holds a Masters of Management and teaches college business/writing courses. Most of her students have no idea that she toils away her hours crafting fictional characters. www.sarahnoffke.com

Check out other work by Sarah author here.

Ghost Squadron:

Formation #1:
   Kill the bad guys. Save the Galaxy. All in a hard day's work.
   After ten years of wandering the outer rim of the galaxy, Eddie Teach is a man without a purpose. He was one of the toughest pilots in the Federation, but now he's

just a regular guy, getting into bar fights and making a difference wherever he can. It's not the same as flying a ship and saving colonies, but it'll have to do.

That is, until General Lance Reynolds tracks Eddie down and offers him a job. There are bad people out there, plotting terrible things, killing innocent people, and destroying entire colonies. **Someone has to stop them.**

Eddie, along with the genetically-enhanced combat pilot Julianna Fregin and her trusty E.I. named Pip, must recruit a diverse team of specialists, both human and alien. They'll need to master their new Q-Ship, one of the most powerful strike ships ever constructed. And finally, they'll have to stop a faceless enemy so powerful, it threatens to destroy the entire Federation.

All in a day's work, right?

Experience this exciting military sci-fi saga and the latest addition to the expanded Kurtherian Gambit Universe. If you're a fan of Mass Effect, Firefly, or Star Wars, you'll love this riveting new space opera.

NOTE: If cursing is a problem, then this might not be for you.

Check out the entire series <u>here.</u>

The Precious Galaxy Series:

Corruption #1

A new evil lurks in the darkness.

After an explosion, the crew of a battlecruiser mysteriously disappears.

Bailey and Lewis, complete strangers, find themselves

suddenly onboard the damaged ship. Lewis hasn't worked a case in years, not since the final one broke his spirit and his bank account. The last thing Bailey remembers is preparing to take down a fugitive on Onyx Station.

Mysteries are harder to solve when there's no evidence left behind.

Bailey and Lewis don't know how they got onboard *Ricky Bobby* or why. However, they quickly learn that whatever was responsible for the explosion and disappearance of the crew is still on the ship.

Monsters are real and what this one can do changes everything.

The new team bands together to discover what happened and how to fight the monster lurking in the bottom of the battlecruiser.

Will they find the missing crew? Or will the monster end them all?

The Soul Stone Mage Series:

House of Enchanted #1:

The Kingdom of Virgo has lived in peace for thousands of years...until now.

The humans from Terran have always been real assholes to the witches of Virgo. Now a silent war is brewing, and the timing couldn't be worse. Princess Azure will soon be crowned queen of the Kingdom of Virgo.

In the Dark Forest a powerful potion-maker has been murdered.

Charmsgood was the only wizard who could stop a

deadly virus plaguing Virgo. He also knew about the devastation the people from Terran had done to the forest.

Azure must protect her people. Mend the Dark Forest. Create alliances with savage beasts. No biggie, right?

But on coronation day everything changes. Princess Azure isn't who she thought she was and that's a big freaking problem.

Welcome to The Revelations of Oriceran. Check out the entire series here.

The Lucidites Series:

Awoken, #1:
Around the world humans are hallucinating after sleepless nights.

In a sterile, underground institute the forecasters keep reporting the same events.

And in the backwoods of Texas, a sixteen-year-old girl is about to be caught up in a fierce, ethereal battle.

Meet Roya Stark. She drowns every night in her dreams, spends her hours reading classic literature to avoid her family's ridicule, and is prone to premonitions—which are becoming more frequent. And now her dreams are filled with strangers offering to reveal what she has always wanted to know: Who is she? That's the question that haunts her, and she's about to find out. But will Roya live to regret learning the truth?

Stunned, #2
Revived, #3

The Reverians Series:

Defects, #1:

In the happy, clean community of Austin Valley, everything appears to be perfect. Seventeen-year-old Em Fuller, however, fears something is askew. Em is one of the new generation of Dream Travelers. For some reason, the gods have not seen fit to gift all of them with their expected special abilities. Em is a Defect—one of the unfortunate Dream Travelers not gifted with a psychic power. Desperate to do whatever it takes to earn her gift, she endures painful daily injections along with commands from her overbearing, loveless father. One of the few bright spots in her life is the return of a friend she had thought dead—but with his return comes the knowledge of a shocking, unforgivable truth. The society Em thought was protecting her has actually been betraying her, but she has no idea how to break away from its authority without hurting everyone she loves.

Rebels, #2

Warriors, #3

Vagabond Circus Series:

Suspended, #1:

When a stranger joins the cast of Vagabond Circus—a circus that is run by Dream Travelers and features real magic—mysterious events start happening. The once orderly grounds of the circus become riddled with hidden threats. And the ringmaster realizes not only are his circus and its magic at risk, but also his very life.

Vagabond Circus caters to the skeptics. Without skeptics, it would close its doors. This is because Vagabond

Circus runs for two reasons and only two reasons: first and foremost to provide the lost and lonely Dream Travelers a place to be illustrious. And secondly, to show the nonbelievers that there's still magic in the world. If they believe, then they care, and if they care, then they don't destroy. They stop the small abuse that day-by-day breaks down humanity's spirit. If Vagabond Circus makes one skeptic believe in magic, then they halt the cycle, just a little bit. They allow a little more love into this world. That's Dr. Dave Raydon's mission. And that's why this ringmaster recruits. That's why he directs. That's why he puts on a show that makes people question their beliefs. He wants the world to believe in magic once again.

Paralyzed, #2
Released, #3

Ren Series:

Ren: The Man Behind the Monster, #1:
Born with the power to control minds, hypnotize others, and read thoughts, Ren Lewis, is certain of one thing: God made a mistake. No one should be born with so much power. A monster awoke in him the same year he received his gifts. At ten years old. A prepubescent boy with the ability to control others might merely abuse his powers, but Ren allowed it to corrupt him. And since he can have and do anything he wants, Ren should be happy. However, his journey teaches him that harboring so much power doesn't bring happiness, it steals it. Once this realization sets in, Ren makes up his mind to do the one thing

that can bring his tortured soul some peace. He must kill the monster.

Note This book is NA and has strong language, violence and sexual references.

Ren: God's Little Monster, #2
Ren: The Monster Inside the Monster, #3
Ren: The Monster's Adventure, #3.5
Ren: The Monster's Death

Olento Research Series:

Alpha Wolf, #1:
Twelve men went missing.

Six months later they awake from drug-induced stupors to find themselves locked in a lab.

And on the night of a new moon, eleven of those men, possessed by new—and inhuman—powers, break out of their prison and race through the streets of Los Angeles until they disappear one by one into the night.

Olento Research wants its experiments back. Its CEO, Mika Lenna, will tear every city apart until he has his werewolves imprisoned once again. He didn't undertake a huge risk just to lose his would-be assassins.

However, the Lucidite Institute's main mission is to save the world from injustices. Now, it's Adelaide's job to find these mutated men and protect them and society, and fast. Already around the nation, wolflike men are being spotted. Attacks on innocent women are happening. And then, Adelaide realizes what her next step must be: She has to find the alpha wolf first. Only once she's located him can she stop whoever is behind this experiment to create wild beasts out of human beings.

Lone Wolf, #2
Rabid Wolf, #3
Bad Wolf, #4